BARNSTORMERS

BARNSTORMERS

DAVID SKIPPER

WALKER BOOKS
AND SUBSIDIARIES
LONDON • BOSTON • SYDNEY

First published 1995 by Walker Books Ltd
87 Vauxhall Walk, London SE11 5HJ

Text © 1995 David Skipper
Cover illustration © 1995 Derek Brazell

2 4 6 8 10 9 7 5 3 1

This book has been typeset in Sabon.

Printed in England

British Library Cataloguing in Publication Data
A catalogue record for this book is available from
the British Library.

ISBN 0-7445-2496-2

CONTENTS

CHAPTER ONE

I guess every town has a haunted house; some dark old building that kids swap stories about in the safe glow of a summer night's campfire. Castleton had Rosethorn Cottage. Hartford had Milehouse Mill. We had Railway Cottage, which was fine enough, I suppose, but it was the Halloway House down river that beat them all and won full marks for scariness. None of us had actually seen the house because it was miles downstream, hidden in a thick patch of forestry land that we thought was difficult to reach by bus or car. But all of us, except Ben, who'd only been with us a month or so, had heard enough stories to paint a pretty good and grim picture of what it would look like. Round our way, the Halloway House was a legend.

First of all, it was October, which is important because autumn draws people closer. In

July, when the nights are hot and the air is clear, you have to shout across the fields for your friends even to notice you. Three months later you're hunched shoulder to shoulder and you whisper. The nights get longer and the wind begins to blow different; full of smoke and mist and the smell of leaves turning to mould under the trees they fell from. By the close of September you're supposed to be through with all the outdoor stuff of picnics and campouts and turning your mind to indoor things like sports halls, swimming pools and youth clubs. I suppose that autumn we'd have done it that way too if everything had been the way it had the year before. But a lot had happened since then.

It was Tyler who mentioned the Halloway House first. We were in the Barn at the time, which wasn't a real barn but an old electronic substation which had been stripped out and abandoned about ten years earlier when a new system was set up in town. "The Barn" was just the easiest thing to call it. It was about half a mile from the river and at the time we'd been going there regularly for about three years.

The Barn wasn't much to look at. Just a brick-built shed, about six metres wide and twice as long. It was old and crumbling and it had a kind of smoky, church-like atmosphere that everybody thought was really cool. In the far left corner of the building there was a

8

small, square brick-built hut, which we called the Office, where we kept all the stuff our parents over the years had told us to throw away for one reason or another; like the home-made ninja throwing stars Cal had made in his first month of metalwork, Tyler's collection of animal skulls and my *2000 AD* comics. At the opposite end of the Barn, the end that faced towards the river, there was a knee-high wooden platform that jutted out from the far wall about a metre or so and ran the full width of the building. On that rotting platform, where a big control desk once stood, was a rusty old table and chairs. The table that, one clear morning two years ago, Cal, Toby and I had hauled out of Oakley Beck. It was around that table that we sat that cold October night. Usually we'd be playing Two's and Eight's or Chase the Ace, or maybe even Top Trumps if the game had got too dull or expensive for Tyler. But that night it was different: the day before, I'd told the Barnstormers (that's the name we got for hanging round the Barn so much) a tale I'd read in a magazine that publishes fantasy and adventure tales. You know the kind of thing: good vs evil, buried treasure, magical worlds with wizards and pirates and unicorns. Over the last year or so I'd gotten into it in a big way. The tale I recounted was about a shy young girl from an ordinary home in an ordinary town who had built a Ouija board – you know, a *weeja* board, one of those alphabet circles they use at séances. In the story the board actually works and, as the glass glides across the board in answer to her question, "What's to become of me?", it spells out the word *princess*. "What do you mean?" asks the girl. *Princess*. "Nonsense!" *Princess*. "No." Angrily the girl throws the glass at the wall which shatters into golden shards of light and the girl, confused and exhausted, falls asleep at the table. She wakes to hazy sunlight streaming through windows she does not recognize – tall, narrow windows cut into thick, grey stone. Then she hears soft tapping on a heavy door and the words, "Your horse is ready for you, Your Highness…"

I told that story on Monday. Later that night I had the Nightmare again. I suppose all the talk of Ouija boards must have sparked it off. Over a year had passed since the day at the lake and I'd dreamt about it so often I'd lost count of the times. The dream itself is pretty much how it happened that day. Except we all seemed so much younger – just little kids. The walk to the lake is the same – all sunny and green, with Tyler singing and Cal cracking jokes and everyone laughing. Colourful is as good a word I can think of to describe it. Me in my red and blue T-shirt that I wore throughout that summer and have never touched since; Kelly close by in her faded jeans, scuffed baseball boots and sweatshirt with ragged cut-off sleeves. As usual, Tyler was sweating it out in his thick yellow Thunderbirds jersey, while up front Cal was yelling at Toby to get on home because he couldn't swim and wasn't coming to the lake and that was that.

I guess the only real difference between the dream and the day is that in the dream it is me, not Cal, who almost reaches Toby in time. He's skimming stones at us and our odd game of two-a-side water polo from the edge of the old wooden footbridge over the "rapids" forty metres away. Then there's a crack. Even over our splashing I can hear it clearly; there's a crack like thunder and the barrier has snapped and Toby is gone. Out of it all, though, the thing that always comes back most clearly about that afternoon is the look on Cal's face.

Toby Calahan was Cal's kid brother.

CHAPTER TWO

The day after I'd told the story about the
princess and the Ouija board, Ben called at my
house. School had been over about an hour
and I was in my bedroom finishing off a chapter of a novel, half reading, half thinking to
myself that what was happening on those
pages was really scary stuff, but you know it's
kind of exciting and maybe ... just maybe if I
ever got the chance to do something as scary
and dangerous myself I'd go ahead and take it.

I get like that sometimes. Maybe everyone
does.

My dad answered the door. He hadn't met
Ben yet because he's usually working, or in his
study listening to old pop music while he glues
kits of model sports cars together. But that
night Mum was at one of her WI meetings in
the church hall down town, so he answered the
door. All my dad said when he met Ben was,

"Hi. I hope you've got a little more sense than the others because I don't see any of them going anywhere fast."

It's true that none of my friends had ever built an Airfix Bugatti, or could understand the lyrics of "A Whiter Shade of Pale" – a weird sixties song that for some reason people over a certain age seem to go misty over – if they did, maybe he'd like them more. But I doubt it. They're all from Greylands over on the south side of town. That's not far, at least not in real terms. But it means that while we have a fancy new house with a two-car garage and big gardens front and back, they live in council houses. Their parents work like dogs just to make ends meet, and mine don't. The rest of the Barnstormers go to the local, over-crowded, undisciplined comprehensive school while I'm stuck at the under-subscribed, over-disciplined Hadrian's Academy for Boys. I can't think of a word strong enough to express how much I hate Hadrian's.

"Come on, let's go, Ben." I hurried downstairs, grabbed my coat and left without even stopping to pull it on. I wanted to get to the Barn, and besides, the less time my dad spent around my friends the better. I know he's an accountant and looking at numbers all day must make you kind of crabby (a double lesson of maths is enough to get me biting the corner of my desk), but I don't see why he has to be rude. None of my friends' parents are like that. Kelly's dad works as a factory security guard and even though he puts in more over-time than my dad, he always takes time to say hello and ask how things are going. A couple of years ago, when Kelly and her mum were out of town visiting a sick relative, he took Cal, Toby and me fishing. Tyler's mum has five children of her own but always manages to find enough room on the kitchen table for three or four more places whenever we call. Ben's parents are great too. His dad is a coun-cil gardener. He moved here when the park he tended down south got turned into a super-market. Cal's mum works part-time at the local bakery and whenever she brings home one of the huge bags full of misshapen and unsold cakes and meringues, she divides it into equal amounts for each of the Barnstormers to take home with them. I have a feeling my dad would sell them to the highest bidder.

Ben and I reached the Barn, which is about a half-mile from my house on the edge of a wide patch of shrubland called the Wilderness, just after six o'clock. It was drawing in dark by then and the Barn was empty. I lit the paraf-fin lamp that hung from the rusty iron rafter which crossed the Barn longways, and moved up to the platform.

And guess what was on the top of the card table!

One Ouija board and, in its centre, one upturned drinking tumbler just like those used by the Greyland Education Authority. Nobody ever owned up to making the board, but I guessed it was Tyler because it wasn't made too well; twenty-six untidy squares of white masking tape with the alphabet written on them in shaky felt-tip, all stuck on to the back of a mouldy old Snakes and Ladders board in a big wobbly circle. Some of the letters were capitals, some weren't. The *p* and the *q* were the wrong way round. I looked at Ben, who simply shrugged and said in agreement, "Tyler."

Twenty minutes later, by which time it was completely dark, everyone had arrived and there we were: Andrew Calahan, Greg Tyler, Kelly Walshaw, Ben Curtis and me, all crammed round this crummy spookboard while, set in the gaps in the walls where dials had once turned, candles cast flickering shadows across the floor.

Five forefingers settled on the glass. Everyone hushed for about a minute and then, because the quiet was scarier than any noise could have been, Tyler began making spooky *Ooooohhhh* sounds, until Cal slapped him up the back of the head and barked at him to be quiet. Tyler's reply was to tell Cal where to go and what to do when he got there (and not in a way that you would talk in front of your

16

mum). When Cal ignored this, Tyler shut up. Tyler was always trying to rattle Cal's cage – you know, the way some people do when they look up to a person they think is cool or talented or special in some way, and can't think of any good way to get their attention. I have a feeling it was because Tyler thought that Cal was everything he was not. At almost thirteen Cal was big; not tall like Ben, but broad and strong-looking and his black, slicked-back hair emphasized what his clothes and manner suggested – tough. Tyler was small for his age, and unlike Cal's angular good looks Tyler was round-faced and sort of cute-looking. His light brown hair, which he'd had close-cropped because he thought it would make him look tougher, only added to the effect. When I first met Greg Tyler he made me think of a lost mongrel puppy. Years later, he still does.

I knew Tyler hated the way he looked, acted, dressed and spoke. But I liked Tyler as much as I liked any of the Barnstormers. We all did. Yet I reckon if anyone of us had actually come out and told him so, Tyler would never have believed anything we told him ever again.

Moths tapped at the window but only the shadow of the glass on the Ouija board moved. Another minute went by. With his free hand Tyler began playing imaginary piano on the table's edge and Cal blew the last mouth-ful of smoke from a filtered Number Six up towards the rafters. When nothing happened after another minute I leaned back in my chair and said as dramatically as I could, "Oh man, this is really great, Ty. We should do this every night – "

"Start up a country league," added Kelly with a grin.

Tyler frowned and that made me giggle. Kelly caught it and soon we were all sniggering. I guess we were all a little spooked. This wasn't like the *magic* Ouija board in the fantasy tale – this was the normal *raising evil spirits* kind. You've probably heard as many stories as we have about séances, with tables lifting into the air and glasses shattering into millions of pieces of razor-sharp shrapnel.

Suddenly, Tyler sat up, pushing out his hands as if stopping traffic, and cried, "Wait!" and his eager, bug-eyed expression alone kept us laughing.

"I just remembered, you've got to spit in the glass."

"Spit?"

"Or ... breathe."

"Breathe." Kelly nodded, picking up the tumbler. So we breathed the glass cloudy and began again.

And this time the tumbler did move.

J was the first letter it glided to, and I suddenly shivered as if a cold gust had blown the door open.

A was the letter the glass then stopped before, wavering a moment, then turning a small circle.

C next, and I looked from the glass to my friends, noticing with a dry swallow that they all looked deadly serious, even Tyler. The glass paused at that letter as if for breath, and then it rattled before shooting fast for: *K*.

I suddenly felt as if someone had punched me. I kind of guessed it was a joke; my mates didn't much worry about hitting below the belt as long as they figured they could bring you round afterwards. But the flickering candles made everything mysterious and shadowy, and I really needed to know for sure. Cal was sitting on my left and I was so wrapped up in what the glass was doing that I didn't notice him move. When his hand slapped on to my leg and his fingers bit into my thigh, I sprang from my chair as if someone had pushed an ejector button.

And the glass kept moving. Fast now, it spelled out the rest of my name. C-R-A-N-D-A-L. And I knew then that the others were pushing it, because they were calling out the letters the glass was heading to before it had reached them.

I swore until I was hoarse and kicked at the chair which had fallen clattering to the platform floor. I felt angry and foolish, and I hated the way Cal was chewing that matchstick like some rebel without a cause. I hated the way he had changed.

"This whole Ouija board thing was a stupid idea and it wouldn't have worked anyway," I moaned.

"I bet it would have worked at the Spook House," whispered Tyler and everyone stopped and looked at him. We all knew what Tyler had meant even though he hadn't mentioned the Halloway House by name. Evidence of the house existed around the Barn in the form of drawings and maps, and one of Kelly's poems, but I don't think any of us had really thought much of the place since before the accident. It was Toby's pet subject really. Round about Hallowe'en he would begin to pester us to take him there and Cal would always say, "Later, Toby. There's plenty of time."

I began to say something, but the old iron door in the corner creaked and I thought I saw something flash past the dirt-speckled square of glass beside it. You know how it is when you catch something out of the corner of your eye, and whatever it is, whether the tiniest of moths or a massive eighteen-wheel tanker on the road in the distance, it's gone before you get the chance to see for sure.

"What was that?"

Four blank faces replied: what was what?

Quickly I tried to wave it away, but Tyler had already caught on and he nudged Cal. "Eh, I think he's spooked, men. Looks like old Crandal's got the willies."

"I *heard* something."

"What was it, Jack?" asked Ben.

"Was it the bogeyman, Jacky?" Tyler grinned. "Is that what you heard. The Booooooogymaaaa—"

"Oh, what do you think, you great big bald baboon?" I growled.

Cal, who had been quietly watching, reached over and pulled out the paperback that had been jutting from the back pocket of my jeans. It was Ray Bradbury's *Something Wicked This Way Comes*. Cal didn't even look at the title before tossing it on the floor as if it were a dead fish that had started to hum. "Well, if you ask me," he shook his head sadly, "I think all this reading has finally warped your mind."

"Jack reads because he writes. That's all," said Kelly, trying to ease the situation. Kelly often did this. Not just for me. For everyone. A few years back, when her dad lost his job at the dairy, Kelly's parents went through a pretty rough patch, shouting at each other and arguing all the time, and Kelly pulled them through it. Now Kelly could sense ripples of tension in the air and smooth them out before

21

anyone knew they were there.

"Yeah," Ben nodded. "Jack's a good writer. He's going to win that competition."

The competition was not my idea. Last month my English teacher, Mr Brennan, called me back after class to congratulate me on a composition I'd written. It was a short fantasy story about a magic amulet that could turn back time and make things right. Mr Brennan reminded me of the inter-school writing competition and of the two hundred pounds prize money and asked if he could enter my story for the school. That night I was going out early with Tyler, to some charity music show he wanted to see at the town hall, and I figured a yes would get me out of the classroom quicker than a no, so I agreed. I didn't think about the prize money. I had no chance of winning. We were up against the top schools in the country.

"Yeah, well, I'm getting worried," Cal continued. "It's not right, just reading all the time. You never used to be like this."

The words "Neither did you" sprang into my head, but I checked them and said with a shrug, "Things change."

Cal's sure expression faded and for a moment I saw the old Andrew Calahan, the one who not so long ago had almost pleaded with me to get him out of the eight hundred metres sports day race because he didn't feel up to it. Then he looked at me coolly and opened his mouth to hit me with some smart remark, but before he could do this, Ben cut in quickly, "Are we gonna do this, or not?" He tapped the board, cleverly faking impatience. "Because if we aren't, I think—"

Cal rose from his chair. His eyes narrowed on Ben. "Nobody's asking you what you think, OK? We don't want your opinion. I don't even know what you're doing –"

"Cal!" Kelly grabbed Cal's arm and eased him back into his seat. I was looking at Ben. Although Cal had not finished his sentence, it was clear that Ben had done so in his head and was upset by what he heard. Even Cal himself seemed sorry now. Kelly's cheeks were flushed and her bright eyes blazed towards Cal. "If we're not bothering to do this," she scraped her chair, ready to stand, "then I'm going home."

Tyler looked at me. "We *are*, aren't we, Jack?"

"Yes," I said. I wasn't in a hurry to raise the dead. I just wanted to change the subject before I said something I'd regret about Cal and his own worrying quirks.

"Well, this is fun," Cal said dryly after we'd been staring down at the glass on the board for about five minutes with nothing happening.

"It's not working very well, is it?" admitted Kelly.

"Maybe it's the board."

"Maybe it's the *glass*," Tyler said defensively.

"Maybe it's the barn."

"I'm sure it would have worked at the Halloway House," repeated Tyler, and there was something in the way he mouthed the last two words that made Ben sit up. The old corrugated door at the far end of the Barn creaked again and I suddenly wished we hadn't doused the paraffin lamp. That rusty old door did sometimes rattle when the wind was howling over the Wilderness, but tonight, although it was cold, there was no wind.

No wind, Jacky. Noooo winnnndddd...

"Don't worry, Jack. It's not a full moon till Sunday."

Tyler guffawed the way he usually did when he thought Cal said something funny. "Yeah, Jack," he sniggered. "Don't worry. I mean, it's no big deal. I used to be a werewolf myself, but I'm all right now-ooooOOOO!"

Lousy joke, OK. But when Tyler leant back and howled, the back legs of his chair slid forwards and he fell crashing backwards, and this seemed to shatter the tension that had been gathering. I tried to hold off laughing by taking a swig of Coke from a can I had taken earlier from the water barrel in the corner, but it went down the wrong way and foam came out of my nose.

By the time Tyler had composed himself, our howling had calmed enough for us to notice a different sound. Quiet rattling from above us. Up on the roof. I glanced from the shadows among the rafters to my friends around the table.

Kelly shrugged.

Without thinking about it, I folded the Ouija board closed. In the short silence that followed, Tyler began pulling his fingers, making them crack. Then the door moved again. This time for sure. This time that rattly old door slammed inward with a deafening bang that rang round the Barn and shook rust from the rafters.

I turned fast and blinked hard. My eyes fixed on the rectangle of blackness where the door had been. There were no monsters in the doorway. No werewolf, ghost or troll. But to me, the three boys that rambled into our Barn seemed somehow worse. There were ways to deal with monsters: silver bullets. Holy water. Garlic. *Conventions.* You followed the right convention, laid down the correct symbol and they wouldn't cross your path. They would do you no harm.

But these! These kids that stood as big and tall and tough-looking as the reputation they worked hard to keep did not follow conventions. They, I realized with a dry swallow, could harm. Often, they did.

I suppose there's a kid like Arnold Corman in every town; the one just a little too smart to be the obvious punk the police keep a close eye on. Arnie didn't have HATE tattooed on to the knuckles of his left hand, but it was there all the same.

He smugly sauntered into the Barn, hands in his jeans, his hair slicked back like Cal's, but not as dark, not as neat. As Richy Singer and Jim Winters followed him in, he turned clumsily and nodded. "Good work, children. You've got this little kindergarten looking really cosy. It's a pity they're about to pull it down."

None of us replied. We all knew that this was a lie. Just one of the tricks Corman used to throw you off balance. I heard Ben whisper something to Tyler, and out of the corner of my eye I saw Tyler smartly elbow him quiet. Mainly though, I was watching Cal as he silently studied Corman. There was something in the way Cal's eyes had become narrow and thoughtful that I didn't like.

"Only I hope you got a grown-up's permission to have all these candles around." He pulled a cigarette from a pack in his back pocket and lit it on the nearest candle. " 'Cause little boys shouldn't play with fire. They get burned."

He grinned stupidly at us, expecting a reply, hoping for something to latch on to. Corman wasn't smart enough to continue without it.

On the wall in front of him was a long corkboard where once, I suppose, when the Barn was still the substation, official notices would have been pinned. Now, instead of safety notices and overtime rotas, it was covered in our stuff: Kelly's sketches, Tyler's theatre play-bills and Cal's old pictures from *Custom Car* and *Motor cycle Weekly*. In front of Corman was an ancient map Cal and I had drawn up for Toby. It showed, as far as we *then* knew, the simplest route from the Barn to the Halloway House. With no argument from us to feed on, Corman scowled at the map and ripped it from the wall. Then he turned and looked at us as if we were insects. "You couldn't find the Halloway House. You little creeps couldn't find a corpse in a coffin."

I'd like to have found *him* in a coffin. He shredded the map, then strode over to the water barrel in the corner and lifted the last two cans out. I'm not sure if it was my senses working overtime, but I thought it was so quiet that I could actually hear the drops of water that were falling from the can, splashing on the concrete like cymbal crashes. Corman tossed one of the cans to Singer and cracked open the one he held. He took one mouthful, then scowled and looked at me as if I'd short-changed him somehow.

"Only two cans. Two stinking cans. What's my friend supposed to do?" He nodded across to Winters, who looked round and dropped a spider he had plucked from a web in the corner. It got a metre away before his boot slid over it. It left a bruise-coloured curve on the concrete.

"You want him to dry up like a prune?"

Silence.

"No." His fist twitched and pumped with frustration. "You wouldn't want that to happen, would you." He was moving towards us now, his icy stare fixed on Tyler, whose fingers were drumming nervously on the can of Coke. With one easy leap Corman was on the platform, looming over us.

"*Would you!*" he screamed at Tyler, who didn't say anything, but his usually rosy cheeks drained their colour. Even in the candle-dimness I could see that.

"I suppose not," I cut in. I hated to say it. It made my insides churn, but I knew Tyler wasn't going to say anything and I figured I better say something before Cal decided to.

"Good." Corman smiled as he plucked the can from Tyler's grasp and tapped him twice on the cheek; the second hard enough to bring the colour back. I flinched and looked at Cal with alarm; his nose was wrinkled as if there was a bad smell in the air, but that was all, and when Corman dropped off the platform and started for the door I breathed the biggest sigh of relief in my life. *They were going.*

Singer and Winters led the way out. Corman turned at the doorway and as a final reminder of who it was that really called the shots, he flashed the stupid, smug grin at each of us. Tyler began studying his fingers keenly, but beside him Cal was returning that same smart grin as if he knew exactly what was ticking over in that twisted little mind of Corman's.

Something in Arnold Corman's grin died a little as he started to go. I thought for one terrible moment that he was going to start something, but he didn't. The back of that leather jacket was the best sight I could have wished for. He was halfway out of the door when I finally allowed myself to breathe easy again, and almost completely through when Cal leaned back in his chair, scratched his ear and as if he were passing some casual remark about the weather, called, "Don't forget to pull the door closed, you pig-eyed pile of horse shit."

CHAPTER THREE

Corman stopped in his tracks and I felt every joint in my body freeze. After that things became a blur.

In my mind the Barn was the old substation again and it was filled with flashing lights and the wailing siren sounds you get in a nuclear power station just before meltdown. Before I knew it I was out of my chair and racing for the corner the way Tyler, Kelly and Ben ahead of me were. Only Cal remained. In the corner of the platform a square had been cut to allow thick electrical piping to run to a transformer outside. All the piping had been stripped out and a tea chest covered the hole. Tyler reached the corner first and shoved the tea chest aside. Corman, meanwhile, had turned in the doorway and was looking at Cal as if he had slapped him. The can he had stolen slipped from his fingers. It spilled its insides over the concrete floor. In the dim light it looked like blood.

"Cal!" I heard myself scream. I felt drunk. Nothing seemed to be happening the way it should. I couldn't understand why Cal had hurled the insult. More than that, I couldn't understand why he wasn't running with us. He *should* have been. That was the law. A convention of our own. If you were prepared to pull something as crazy as what Cal had just done, then you had to follow the rules of combat. And the rule in this case was run.

I yanked Cal out of the chair, screaming at him to get moving, and heard something rip as I dragged at his jacket. This sound seemed to break whatever spell Cal was under, because after that he clicked into gear. Tyler, Kelly and Ben had already vanished down the gap as Cal and I reached the corner and as I dived into the blackness I heard Corman shrieking at Winters and Singer to go round the back. Corman didn't know that the duct was L-shaped and ran down a little way into the ground below the Barn and came out about a hundred metres to the *side*.

The duct was narrow, dark and scary. I could hear sounds over our fast breathing – scratching sounds, as if there were rats down there. But I couldn't see a thing. I knew that Ben was somewhere up ahead of me, but I didn't know how close. Then suddenly, at another scratching sound, he jolted. His foot kicked out and caught my jaw, sending what felt like a sharp electric shock running along the right side of my face. My whole mouth was numb and my hands and knees were raw when I finally followed him out of the duct. Standing in the fresh air at last we suddenly realized how dusty it had been down there in the duct and began rubbing our eyes and coughing. But we didn't hang around. As soon as Tyler and Kelly helped Cal out we were racing across the Wilderness towards the building at the end of it. It was Walmslow Juniors. Our old primary school.

For some way behind I heard somebody yelling, but I could only guess it was Corman. I was racing so fast I was in danger of turning a somersault. I couldn't have looked back even if I'd wanted to. Tyler was in front, with Ben and Kelly close behind him. Cal was beside me, easily matching my pace, stride for stride. I knew that even though his keenness for all things sporting had long since died (any interest he now showed in speed was purely mechanical) he could still have raced on ahead, and as ill-timed as the moment was, I felt glad he had chosen not to. Cal knew that I was not a good runner. Short sprints I can cope with. Anything over two hundred metres and I feel like dying. The old school seemed a mile away. I knew I wouldn't be able to keep this pace for long. My throat felt raw and my heart was beating a drum solo in my chest. A feeling similar to sea-sickness was beginning to sweep over me. I only hoped our pursuers were feeling as lousy as I was.

Tyler was slowing too. In the beginning he had been just a dark shape in the distance. Now we had caught him and Cal slowed to pull him along. We reached the shadowy playground breathless and aching, but managed through years of practice to vault the nearly chest-high fence easily: nobody uses school gates except when a teacher on morning patrol is nearby.

The Barnstormers' new school in Greylands is a big, modern comprehensive, but this (the one we all shared before I got banished to Hadrian's) was just a single storey and more widely spread, built in blocks joined by long narrow corridors. The cafeteria, gym and classroom blocks all zigzagged out from the main hall like the black bits of some massive 3D crossword puzzle, and provided plenty of dark corners to squat out of sight. We'd used it often enough in the past for that reason.

Back in the Wilderness I could hear Corman screeching like an Indian from a TV western, whooping out war cries, but still we didn't stop running and we didn't look back.

When I was five years old I drank from a bottle of pink, sweet-smelling window cleaning fluid and had to have my stomach pumped, but I didn't feel as sick as I did right then.

At the main hall Ben, who was some way ahead of us, carried on towards the staff room. The rest of us took a sharp left towards the rose garden at the back of the art room. By then Cal was just about having to drag Tyler along. Before we turned round the art block I managed a glance backward and saw three dark shapes leaping the fence.

"Hurry," I gasped and pushed Tyler from behind. Kelly reached the rose garden first and easily jumped the little stone wall that surrounded it. A moment later, too hurried to be cautious, the rest of us dived into the thin patch of evergreens growing beyond the wall.

It had rained earlier and almost immediately the damp from the soil we were squatting in seeped into our clothes. I could hear Tyler's hoarse breathing and the rustle of some old crisp packets caught in a kind of mini whirlwind in the lower school doorway, but I heard nothing of Corman. I'm not sure how long we crouched there, not moving, not daring to do or say anything. It might have been only five minutes, but it felt like twenty-five. I was thinking about Ben. I hoped he was safe.

Finally, Cal got to his knees, rubbed dirt from his hands and sniffed, "No sweat."

"No sweat!" I cried. I can't tell you how mad I was. First of all we didn't know where

Ben was, whether he was lost or being used as a life-sized punch bag. I was feeling like I'd just gone three times round the world's worst rollercoaster and here we were, kneeling like pigs in a pen, all gunged up with cold wet clay and slugs and snails, and our hearts still pounding hard enough to burst.

"No sweat," I repeated, but was so mad the words caught in my throat and came out little more than a whimper. "You nearly got us killed, you idiot. All you had to do was keep your mouth shut for five more seconds and Corman would have waltzed out of the Barn thinking he'd just done something clever. You know that. What the hell are you trying to –"

Cal's hand shot towards me so fast I was suddenly reminded of the day we met. That day he split my lip for some reason I can't remember now. I'm sure I deserved it. I've never known Cal hit anyone without good cause. I was only seven at the time so I suppose I was being pretty obnoxious. Most seven-year-olds can be at times.

But this time Cal didn't slug me. His hand clamped over my mouth and he pulled me down, nodding to the art room wall. Three horribly twisted shadows spilled over the brickwork like ink.

Singer and Winters dropped on to the wall in front of us, so close I could have reached up and punched them if I'd wanted to. With this thought in mind I flashed a warning look at Cal. He returned a resentful frown as if to say that he wasn't *that* stupid. I just wasn't sure any more. Thankfully Corman himself wasn't close enough. He was pacing and swearing and spitting out threats somewhere on the pavement in front. I couldn't see exactly where, but I could tell by his voice that he was close.

I'm gonna get him for this. I'm gonna get even. He'll pay. They'll be sorry.

Winters leaned against the bush I was under and icy water that had been trapped on the leaves showered down my neck. It was like an electric shock. I don't know how I held down the scream. I was angry, depressed, humiliated, soaked and scared, and it wasn't even eight o'clock. I felt like screaming good and loud.

Corman and his apes moved on about five minutes later when the cold drizzle began again.

"Well, that was a pretty stupid thing you did back there in the Barn," I said as I climbed to my feet, squeezing water out of my shirt and brushing dirt from my trousers.

"Oh, Arnold Corman doesn't scare me." Cal waved my grouch away as if it were nothing. "I'm not scared of anything any more."

Tyler look at him curiously. "Not even the

Halloway House? I mean, not even after the terrible thing that happened there all those years ago?"

Cal shook his head. "I'm not scared of *anything*," he repeated.

"Yeah," I replied. "I know. That's what worries me." But Cal hadn't heard. He had already leapt over the wall and was moving out into the dark of the playground.

We found Ben sitting in the bike sheds of the upper school at the end of the street. Probably as a peace gesture to me, Cal asked Ben if he was OK. (Cal wasn't happy when Ben started tagging along with us, and to begin with I had a hard time just getting Cal to acknowledge him.)

Ben nodded in surprise.

"Come on," said Cal. "I want to see Lightning."

We followed Cal to the rear entrance. There, he glanced over his shoulder into the darkness of the playing field and the little squares of yellow light from the houses beyond it. When it was clear that nobody else was around, he dug a hand deep into his pocket.

We weren't actually breaking in. At least that's what Cal reckoned. Technically, if you don't damage anything, it's different.

During county sports day, when the rest of the school was out cheering its only hope of a medal (a kid called Penguin Peters because of the odd way he ran), Cal sneaked into the staffroom and took a plasticine print of the key. Next day in metalwork he filed down a larger key until it sat neatly into the cast he had made. Now Cal often used the key to sneak into the workshop and look in on Lightning.

The key fitted perfectly and turned without a sound. I had been in the new school only twice before; last year to see the Christmas show in which Tyler played the Tin Man in the *Wizard of Oz* brilliantly. (Tyler was nuts about musical shows and it always amazed me how someone so timid and shy around strangers had the guts to stand in front of an audience and do the stuff most of us wouldn't do to save our lives.) The second time was when the school first got Lightning. That was at Easter. Back then it was just a heap of rusted metal. I couldn't believe that the school had actually paid good money for it.

I really wasn't interested in seeing Lightning again, but there's something exciting about being in school after dark, in the same way that there's a thrill about being out of school when you're supposed to be there, so I tagged along anyway.

A school at night is a bit like a museum. The air is cool and quiet and everything is colourless and shadowy. You whisper even though you know that the chance of anyone other than the caretaker being there is slim.

Even in the darkness it was easy to tell how different Greyland Comprehensive was to my school. Instead of polished stone and waxed wood panelling, the corridors were spatter-painted walls and scuffed and curling linoleum. Any words on the walls of Hadrian's corridors were on special plaques celebrating the people our teachers thought important: Darwin. Einstein. Newton. Pasteur.

The walls of Greylands were scratched with names the kids thought special in some way; they were mainly pop groups and TV stars. Over the door to the metalwork room some-body had scrawled the name of the latest heavy metal sensation. Tyler said they were crap. Tyler often used that word. That or "brilliant", depending on how he felt.

Because of some weird rule about forges and schoolboys, introduced last year when a kid called Joey Camberwell spilled molten metal on to the linoleum and caused a fire alert, the doors of the metalwork room had to lock. Only the Porta-store tool cabinet was securely fastened, so entering the workshop was no problem.

The smell of burnt oil and grease hits you as you push through the doors. Tiny slivers of scrap metal (what the teachers call "swarf") sparkle between the big dark shapes that in the daytime are lathes and drills and saws. Lightning was behind all these. Tucked away in the corner where it had been the last time I'd seen it. But that was about the only thing that remained the same. It was not the hopeless mass of flaking paint and rust I remembered. It was the sleek, cool-looking motor cycle Cal had imagined it could be the day, six months ago, when he had spotted it in the corner of Junkyard Joe's. The yard, of course, like all junkyards, had a big Alsatian and a strict policy of NO TRESPASSING. But Cal had gotten to know Joe (and the dog) quite well since the day, two years earlier, he first wheeled in his bicycle looking for a set of dérailleur gears when at his age he had no business knowing what something as technical as dérailleur gears are. We hadn't been looking for anything in particular the day Cal spotted Lightning, simply cutting through on our way to the sports centre ice-rink. But when Cal saw the bike, leaning against the shell of an old yellow Escort, our whole plan changed and we spent the entire morning tracking down Cal's metalwork teacher, who had been looking for a suitable project for the school.

We never got to the ice-rink. Tyler never got to cut sprays of ice over the older girls who would first be angry, then would pinch his cheek and remark how sweet he looked. Cal never got to chat up the pretty redheaded girl who sold us frothy coffee and hot dogs in the coffee bar and I never got to hold Kelly's hand doing a chain flip. That day I really hated Lightning. But there have been times since then, when I'd seen Cal at the end of the day, covered in oil and grease, looking tired but contented, when I've been glad it's been there. The only thing that worried me was that Cal might become too attached to it. Even after all the work he had put in, Lightning still belonged to the school, and because Greylands, like most other schools, had been hit with cash cuts, there had been talk of selling stuff: an auction at the Hallowe'en open day had been rumoured.

Now, in the thin light cutting through the school window, the chrome gleamed like silver and the petrol tank exploded with the bright new colours of a deep red sunset. Tyler carefully ran his hand over the polished black leather seat as if he were stroking a fine horse, and said, "Brilliant."

"I know it looks OK, but the engine still needs work," murmured Cal as we were heading past the bright takeaway houses at the end of town; the Indian that smelt of curry and the Chinese that smelt of seaweed. Town way wasn't the quickest route home, but it's light when the nights are dark and sheltered when the wind begins to cut. Round about October we start heading into town; normally later than we did that night because there's often a reluctance to go home until something has happened. If you've been run off the school roof by the security guard or you've managed to send the weather-vane above the church spinning with one good whack of a stone, you feel as if you've achieved something, however small. I guess that Friday the achievement was simply getting through with our limbs intact. We didn't hang around long.

CHAPTER FOUR

The weekend went without hassle. But then everything we did seemed geared away from Corman and his gang. On Saturday afternoon, instead of hanging around the arcade opposite Tiltson's motor bike shop, we did something we hadn't for a while. We went skating. The frothy coffee at the ice-rink tasted the same even though it cost more, and apart from the fact that something awful had happened to the hot dogs they sold at the coffee bar, nothing else seemed to have changed. Kelly was still a whizz on the ice. Tyler couldn't stop showing off. Cal spent most of the time talking to the girl behind the coffee bar counter and I had to look after Ben, who hadn't been on the ice before.

We spent Sunday ripping weeds and brambles from Kelly's gran's garden. The garden backs on to the railway. It's very long and since Kelly's grandfather died last year it had become wildly overgrown. What we thought would be an easy hour's work turned out to be a full day's graft. Throughout the day Kelly's gran pottered in and out with mugs of tea and trays of home-made cake and sandwiches. When it became too dark to work any more we stacked everything we had collected into a corner ready to burn next week when the wood had dried. There's nothing better, said Mrs Walshaw, than hot potatoes baked in the ashes of an open fire. Walking home, Kelly informed us that earlier in her life, her gran had been something of a gipsy.

That night I was asleep before I had time to think about the day at the lake.

There were no nightmares.

Because of a tradition that started so long ago that nobody could remember exactly how, we never met on Mondays. When I reached the Barn after tea on Tuesday, the door was open, the lamp was burning and Tyler was standing in the middle of the floor, scratching his cheek as he looked from one shadowy corner to another.

"Something," he said, "isn't right." When I asked him *what* wasn't right he just shrugged. I noticed that a pile of old paperbacks in the corner had toppled over, but I couldn't be sure if that hadn't happened during our visit from Corman. The shredded pieces of our map to the Halloway House still lay where they had fallen.

Kelly arrived about ten minutes later, wearing jeans and an old pink sweatshirt which on anyone else might have looked plain. Her hair, which for years she had kept tied back in a short pony tail, now flowed like silk. In the lamplight it seemed to glow. Under one arm she carried a musty old book the size of a large cereal packet. At school that day she and Tyler had been telling Ben more about the Halloway House and the terrible thing that happened there. How old man Halloway, one cold October night not so long ago, had murdered his wife and step-children. The book, which had been Kelly's grandfather's, told the history of our county, including an entire chapter on our town and the forestry land further down river where the Halloway House stands.

When Cal turned up, later than usual, we gathered around the table on the platform and opened the book. It contained lots of faded photographs of people dressed in old-fashioned working clothes, standing outside factory gates or sitting on the steps of street houses that looked old even back then. One picture showed a group of five ragged children sitting on top of a footbridge over a stream. I thought they looked a little like us. Four boys and a girl out for adventure. Victorian kids were big on adventure. *The Railway Children* and all that stuff. These days most kids have video games instead.

I figured it was going to be one of Tyler's weird nights. First of all there was that "Something isn't right" business. And now, every time we turned a page with a map or picture of the river, he would look over his shoulder as if someone might be spying, then whisper, "I went to the river last night." Because we *all* figured it was one of Tyler's weird nights and knew he was dying for someone to ask him why, nobody did.

The centre pages of the book were taken up by a map of our town and its outskirts. Apart from our own crude sketches, which were obviously way out of scale, I hadn't seen a map of our town before, and I couldn't believe how close everything was. Places I thought were miles away were simply out of sight, hidden by some building, tree line or hill. Even Ben said that the Halloway House, which crouched in the top right corner of the map like a spider on a cobweb, didn't seem as far as we'd led him to believe. We were all small town kids. I'd never realized that before.

"It's not that the house is so far," Kelly explained. "It's that it's difficult to get to. It was the forester's place. The whole area is overgrown. There's no good road."

"Then what's that?"

"The river. The river cuts through the woods."

"I was at the river on Monday!" Tyler said, less casually. Then, when we ignored him again, he jerked up his head and looked towards the far side of the Barn. "What was that?"

We looked at him wearily.

"I heard something."

I remembered how our last spill with Corman had started. This sounded a little familiar to me and I smelled a rat. Of course Tyler looked serious, but Greg Tyler could spin you a lie better than anyone I've ever known. I don't think he had ever taken the blame for anything he had done wrong in his life. He'd just sort of slip into another character, level his gaze at you and say something like, "It wasn't me. I was nowhere near it. I've been in Harper's Woods all day looking for brambles." After that, the more you'd press him, the more detailed his story would get, until in the end you'd swear that Tyler really had spent the day looking for brambles in Harper's Woods. But this time I wasn't buying it.

"So what do you think it is, Greg?" I sneered. "Mad Man Halloway come to warn us away from his haunted house?"

Tyler looked at me as if I'd gone insane. He turned to Ben.

"It came from the office. Didn't you hear it?"

Ben shook his head. Kelly and Cal said, "No."

Swearing we all needed our ears washing out, Tyler scraped out of his seat, then strode, first purposefully and, as he approached, more cautiously, towards the brick shed in the corner. Pretty much as I'd expected, Tyler gasped as he disappeared into the office. Then there was a moment's silence, followed by papers flying and something crashing to the ground. When the mood took Tyler to be dramatic, it did so in a big way. Any moment now his arm would appear round the corner and he would pretend to strangle himself.

The arm didn't appear.

There was a long silence, then Tyler quietly and undramatically stepped out of the office, his cheek and shirt smeared with blood. It was not ketchup and not paint, I realized instantly. Real blood has a colour all its own – darker than you think and quite unmistakable. I've never seen a fake blood that can match it.

My first thought was that someone had been in the office; that Tyler had been attacked. His bloody cheek had drawn attention away from his arms, which I now noticed were folded together as if he were holding a baby.

It was not a baby.

Tyler carefully carried the bundle over to us.

"It's a fox," said Kelly.

"It must have crawled in through the duct after we moved the chest the other night."

Tyler nodded. "Look at its paw."

As the creature trembled in Tyler's arms I saw the dark blood that was drying on the matted fur of its front leg.

Tyler brought the fox closer. He had no trouble carrying it. It wasn't an adult. The fox was not much bigger than Kelly's gran's tabby cat. Its white muzzle was rounded, not long and sharp like that of a mature animal. The soft whines it gave out were like those of a frightened puppy.

Tyler seated himself on the edge of the platform and cradled the fox, humming soothingly to it as Cal, using Tyler's penknife, cut two strips off his own T-shirt and cleaned the wound with a strip dampened with water from the barrel in the corner, and bandaged it with the other strip. The cut wasn't as bad as we had thought. It wasn't poisoned and there was no glass in it. By the time Cal had finished cleaning its paw the fox understood that we were not going to harm it and lost its frightened look. But it still appeared exhausted and starving and we had nothing to feed it.

We all had good reasons why we couldn't take the fox home, but all of us agreed that, for tonight at least, it really shouldn't be left alone. So, as if we were simply deciding whose turn it was to go to the off-licence for crisps, and cola, we did this: Cal picked up the pack of cards we kept in the corner of the platform next to the table. He shuffled them quickly and as we gathered around the table, he dealt us one card each. I turned my card over first. The last time we'd done this I got a king and sat back and enjoyed the suspense. This time I got a seven. An OK card. Plenty of cards below a seven. Kelly turned over a jack. Tyler an eight. Ben tapped the table nervously before swallowing hard and revealing a king. Casually, Cal shrugged and flipped over his card. Another seven. A two man play-off: Cal shuffled the pack again and we both took a card. I took a jack. Cal took a king.

CHAPTER FIVE

The catch clicked as I pushed open the door and that ruined any chance of sneaking in unnoticed, so to stop anyone from peering round the doorway to see what was up, I stomped around in a play of wiping my feet, called out, "It's only me," then charged upstairs as quickly as I could.

By this time the fox had become so comfortable in my arms that it had fallen asleep. I placed it on the old bean bag in the corner of my room, then went downstairs and made myself cream cheese and beefy crisp sandwiches. I was starving. Four o'clock next morning, the fox decided that it was starving too.

When my alarm clock rang three hours later I was even more dazed than usual. (It had taken me ages to find something the fox would eat rather than play with, then after that I took it out to the garden the way you do after a meal with a puppy that isn't properly house-trained. The fox itself looked like a puppy, small and timid, yet just trusting enough with the person who had given it food and shelter and cared for its hurt paw, to stay rather than bolt. Perhaps it was too young to go it alone. At one point it did begin to limp its way to the broken hedge at the back of the garden, but I wasn't worried. If the fox had bolted, that would have been fine with me.)

I staggered downstairs like a zombie and before I'd even set foot in the kitchen I was strafed with questions for which I had no answers. Right then, I was so woozy, if you'd asked me which way the sky was, I'd have pointed every way but up.

"You were down here last night, weren't you? You drank the last of the milk I put aside for breakfast. And where's the broccoli quiche I made for the church bazaar? You can't have eaten it all. It was enormous."

I was stumped. The broccoli quiche was enormous. I wished Dad hadn't left so early. He might have bailed me out. The seconds ticked away and it was clear Mum really wanted answers.

"I..." I began. "I feel ... sick." I coughed twice automatically and tried to remember how I used to make myself look feverish on the mornings Mad Mr Mason was due to throw one of his maths tests. "Can I have an aspirin? I have a headache."

I got the hand on the forehead test, two Junior Disprin and instructions to stay in bed. Twenty minutes later Mum left for work.

When I was sure she had gone I slipped into my old clothes and dashed out. I hoped a teacher from Hadrian's didn't drive past. If I was spotted strolling back from the shops in ripped denims, carrying two bacon and egg quiches and a giant can of Pedigree Chum, I'd have a lot of explaining to do. Our dog died two years ago.

"Hi, Jack."

I couldn't believe it; a hundred yards from home and I'd been caught. But then I realized that I hadn't. Mr Williams *was* a teacher. He lived at the end of our street, in one of the smaller houses that curve on to Maple Drive. But, fortunately, he wasn't one of my teachers. Mr Williams taught maths at Greylands. He smiled and then eyed the dog food curiously.

"How are you finding Hadrian's?" He began piling tattered textbooks into the boot of his car. I didn't want to be rude, so I simply shrugged.

"In five years' time, come exam-time," he said, "you will appreciate it."

Five years!

"Have you seen Andrew lately?"

"Cal?"

"Yes. I was wondering how he is."

I looked at him blankly.

"He hasn't been in school for some time now. Tonsilitis, I believe. Is that right, Jack?"

Cal had his tonsils taken out when he was nine. The day after, I visited him in hospital. His throat looked like chopped liver. I was almost sick.

"Oh, yeah," I said. "He's been really bad."

"Cal's a bright boy, but he can't afford to let things slide. He lost too much ground last year." Mr Williams' gaze lost its focus for a moment. "He seemed to be improving, but lately his attendance has become worse. You're his friend, Jack. How does he appear to you?"

"It's never been easy to figure out Cal."

Mr Williams nodded. "He isn't having any problems at home, is he?"

I said, "His parents," without thinking, then stopped. It's kind of an unwritten rule that you don't discuss your friends with outsiders. But I really wanted to talk to someone. Having lost one son, Cal's folks had decided that whatever happened, they weren't going to lose another. Last week Cal cut his hand, hardly more than a scratch, on a piece of Lightning he had taken home to work on in his shed. Mrs Calahan almost needed sedation. Next day she bought a first aid manual and three different kinds of antiseptic. It's a bit like my family in reverse.

"They're just a little over-protective at the moment. It's not what Cal needs."

"Well, if he needs to talk to somebody, tell him I'm here. OK?"

"OK."

The fox was still sleeping when I got back. I left it Rynn's old drinking bowl full of fresh water and half the bacon and egg quiche, then dashed out again.

I reached Greylands about ten minutes later.

All the streets in the estate look pretty much the same; kind of *tired*, as if they were once respectable, but after years of neglect have finally given up. On most of the houses the paintwork had started to peel, and even on dry days the brickwork seemed damp and crumbling. Where there were grass verges, they were either dug away, or overgrown and littered with used cans and sweet wrappers. A lot of the paving was cracked and weedy.

Mangy dogs, like oversized rats, roamed everywhere.

Cal's house was smarter than most. Mrs Calahan had built a kind of rockery in the tiny front garden from the whitewashed bricks Cal, Toby and I had collected from a building site years ago. We'd planned to build a castle, but never quite got there.

As I reached Cal's house and moved up the path, I heard the click of the door-catch and quickly dived behind the garden shed. If it was Cal's mum, in her now normal state of worry, she'd wonder what I was doing there when both Cal and I ought to have been in school. If she began to fuss, Cal would get angry and there'd be an argument. I didn't want that.

When I saw that it was Cal, I fell into step with him as he passed the shed. He didn't look round at me, but as we strode along the street, he said, "You know, jumping out on people like that may be fine over High Grange way, Jack. But round here it's not very smart. Mr Bedlington has a shotgun."

"I wanted to surprise you."

"Yeah, well you did. Shouldn't you be at school?"

"Me!" I said quickly and my voice turned into a girlish shriek.

I took a deep breath. "Look, I just saw Mr Williams. He was asking about you. Said you have *tonsilitis*. Is that right? Are you really the first person in the world to grow a second set?"

"Williams is a pain."

Mr Williams was not a pain. Any teacher would have given up on Cal a long time ago. Last month, in his class, Cal poured a bottle of Indian ink over a kid called McCarthy when he called him a nutcase. Mr Williams sent McCarthy to the swimming-pool showers to wash and cool off, and kept the incident quiet.

Cal narrowed his eyes at me.

"Since when did you get so friendly with teachers, Jack?"

"You're skipping school again, you moron," I cried. "Williams is OK, but you can only push him so far. After that he'll have to get in touch with social services. It's his job."

We continued walking in silence; past the red brick of St Michael's, past the plate glass of the newsagent and community centre and the old corner grocer's that is now a video rental store. I was beginning to think that after the "moron" remark, Cal had written me out of the day completely, then finally, without looking round or slowing, he said, "OK."

Right then, that was more than enough.

At the end of the street Cal turned right, which I knew was the short cut through the back of the shops to the school and Eton Road beyond it.

Cal gave me a sideways glance. "Satisfied?"

I nodded dumbly.

"What about you? Is your Little Lord Fauntleroy outfit in the wash?"

The uniform for Hadrian's is dark green trousers and blazer trimmed with yellow, white shirt and striped school tie. I thought about lying for a moment, then said, "*I'm* ditching school." This time Cal didn't flinch, but I added, "The fox ... you know," as if to explain.

We moved on to Marchant Street, then cut a sharp left through the narrow alley behind the Co-op and Tiltson's. Something was bothering me, and it wasn't that we were passing the motor bike shop.

"Why didn't the others tell me you were skipping school?"

"They think you worry too much."

I almost laughed but the sound of the rear door to Tiltson's opening then scraping closed, checked it. I knew who haunted Tiltson's bike shop, and before the first word was even called I knew from the heavy footsteps who it was shouting at us to stop.

I was prepared to run. I looked at Cal, ready to take my cue from him. "Relax," he said. "Everything is under control." As I copied Cal and looked back I saw figures, like a solid wall, spread across the alleyway.

Corman, Winters, Singer and some kid in a biking jacket who I hadn't seen before. He looked younger than his mates – our age, I guessed.

Corman, chugging beer from a small dark bottle, strolled up to us. Three paces behind, the others followed. I remembered Corman's threat, *I'm gonna get him for this. I'm gonna get even...* and saw that although he appeared calm, his free hand was clenched. I hoped Cal would keep his cool; with the crazy way he'd been acting lately, it was by no means certain.

Some way off I heard a dog bark. Another joined it and then I realized that the dogs weren't playing, they were fighting. The kid in the biking jacket laughed nervously as Cal and Corman stared at each other. It was Corman who spoke first. Two simple words:

"It's mine."

Cal blinked four times, fast. A nervous thing he hadn't done since we were little kids. "What?"

"You know what, stupid. The bike. The motor cycle." Corman looked back at his friends. "By the end of the month it will be mine."

I remembered the rumour of the Hallowe'en open day auction and looked urgently at Cal, unsure of what he was thinking. He appeared to be in control. He had stopped blinking. His hands hung easily at his side.

Mine weren't. My hands were suddenly clenched so tightly they hurt. I knew what Lightning meant to Cal. It was the only thing he had taken a real interest in since Toby's death. All the things he had shown enthusiasm for before – swimming, music, football – had been washed away as part of a past he seemed loath to remember. But Lightning was different.

Lightning was something special. Something new.

Arnold Corman was taller than Cal by a

good eight centimetres. Cal was taller than me. But I pushed my way between the two of them as if they were nursery school kids, and angrily shoved my hands hard at Corman's chest. Taken by surprise, he toppled back towards the wall. The bottle he'd been holding cracked against it and beer foamed over the brickwork. Corman was left clutching a jagged piece of glass as sharp and sturdy as a large kitchen knife. In confusion he looked from me to his friends with shocked disbelief. The new kid took a step back as Corman was scrambling to his feet. The kid looked scared – as if he wanted to run, but was fighting the urge.

I didn't feel anything, apart from a slight dizziness. I noticed that blood was dripping from Corman's hand. With a splat, a drop hit an old yellow newspaper on the ground. I thought I was going to faint; Corman was coming at me with a broken bottle, Winters and Singer were screaming, "Kill him, kill him," and all I could do was faint.

But I didn't.

An incredible noise cut through my dizziness. A noise that was at the same time sharp and deep and unbelievably loud. As I put my arms out to steady myself, I thought it must be a police loud-hailer. Then I realized that it was simply that someone had shouted. Maybe the shape of the alley made Cal's voice boom louder than any of us had expected; powerful enough to stop Corman in his tracks. "TOUCH HIM OR THE MOTOR BIKE AND I WILL KILL YOU!"

Despite the threat, Corman did touch the motor bike, but that was some time later.

Things cooled off remarkably quickly after Cal's outburst. Although acting fierce, Corman was easily pulled away by Singer and Winters. Cal, as far as I know, went on to school and I dashed home to check the fox. I wondered just how injured it actually was. When I'd taken it into the garden the night before it had moved very slowly and shakily and it never put its cut paw on the ground. I remembered that when Rynn got sick a visit to the vet cost a packet. I shambled home wondering whether you got some kind of discount if the animal was wild.

Most of the water from the bowl I'd left had sloshed on to the floor. The spill had run along the grooves in the corduroy carpet to my library books and was seeping into the opened pages. Only half the quiche had gone. The rest had been nuzzled over the skirting and into most of the carpet. Right then the floor looked like one of those weird modern art paintings that make you dizzy if you stare at it too long. There were little yellow paw marks everywhere. I think the fox must have been trying

63

to pick out the bacon pieces, while leaving the egg. If *I'd* done that I would have got a lecture on how there were millions of starving people in the world who'd be glad of a little protein.

The fox wasn't on the bean bag.

It wasn't on the bed, or under it.

Backtracking, I realized what I had done. Shutting doors is just something I never think of. Not unless my parents are in a particularly crabby mood, or they're playing some bad sixties music I want to shut out. The grandfather clock in the living-room chimed the half hour and I sighed. It was not even ten o'clock and already it was bad news all round.

Lightning was going to be sold off, I'd just written myself on to Corman's death list and somewhere in the house, a wild animal was at large.

The auction, I found out later, *was* to be held at the school; during the open day on the last Sunday in the month. That gave anyone interested in any of the items to be auctioned just over two weeks to raise the cash.

In the Barn that night we pooled our money (fifteen pounds and seventy pence) and sat round the table trying to think up some ways of raising more. I groaned at each bad suggestion. I was in a stinking mood. At other times I might have been our best asset; able to ask my parents to help out. But right then, after what the fox had done, all I could promise was a big fat useless IOU that I probably wouldn't be able to make good until around my thirtieth birthday. My pocket money had been axed only three hours earlier when my dad came home to find the model Rolls Royce Silver Ghost he'd spent every wet weekend for a year building in as many pieces as the expensive kit had first contained.

I had found the fox in the kitchen, peering out of the waste bin next to the fridge like a furry glove puppet, blackcurrant jam smeared over its snout, a strip of banana skin hanging from one ear. It must have already ransacked Dad's study and demolished the Rolls. The perfect little steering wheel was jutting from the side of its mouth like a child's dummy.

It's hard to describe the horror I felt. It took my breath away. I guess it must be like diving into a freezing river, knowing the chill is going to kill you, the only question is when.

I lunged for the fox before it could do any more damage and realized that whatever problem it had had with its paw, it was now resolved. It sprang from the bin as if a hungry pack of hounds were behind it.

Eventually I captured the animal by closing every door in the house, cornering it in the living-room and slowly boxing it in with the furniture so that it didn't know which way to run. After that, using some hidden store of patience, I carried the little monster in my unfastened sportsbag to the start of the Wilderness and set it free. And now, six hours later, as Cal and Kelly and Tyler and Ben and I racked our brains trying to figure out what to do about Lightning, the fox was strutting around the Barn as if it owned the place. Wily as a fox, isn't that what they say? It remembered the Barn. It remembered the pipe duct. I guess in its cunning little foxy head, it remembered it quite liked it there.

" 'Suppose we could sell something," sniffed Tyler. He was sitting at the table next to me, clacking together two little rectangular magnets he'd prized out of an old cassette player that he had pulled from the river the day before. I wondered out loud if there was anywhere we might be able to sell a fine quality fox fur, and Kelly, at my other side, thumped my arm so hard it made my fingers tingle. I didn't mind the ache. As she leant over I caught a smell of something soft and flowery. I was surprised at how sweet it was. Before this, all other perfume I'd smelt had seemed about as sweet as fly killer. Mrs Rawlings, my old biology teacher, could clear a barn of wasps in ten seconds flat.

"Sorry," I said, working the feeling back into my fingertips. "I like him really. He's one cute fox," I added quickly and Kelly grinned and the others sniggered. I don't know why.

Sometimes I speak too fast and get my words all muddled. Maybe I did that. Ben put in the suggestion of washing some cars, and Tyler, fresh out of old Mr Lemcur's modern history lesson, developed this crazy idea of weaving old bits of wool into something we could sell, just like they did in the old days. After that whacky scheme talks broke down completely. Truth is, there are really only a handful of good money making ideas in the unwritten *Kids' Book of Modern Living*, and they didn't take much thinking about. All we could do, we decided, was to give them all a try.

We left the Barn earlier than usual. Tyler said he had somewhere to go, and Ben wanted to see a programme about seabirds on TV.

I went home to more trouble. This time from Mum. I tried to explain about the fox and got angry when she wouldn't listen. Finally, I got sent to my room, which was where I was going anyway. As I was tidying up I spotted, jutting out from the shadowy no-man's-land under my bed, something I'd forgotten about – my five year diary. It was red and black and had a picture of Dennis the Menace on the cover. I'd been given it for my ninth birthday and had used it regularly for almost three years. Then I read the *Diary of Anne Frank* and after that everything I had to say seemed too trivial to document.

I picked up the diary, which was, like

Dennis' jumper, striped red and black, but over those lines were added teeth marks and sticky fox spit. I wiped the book on the bottom corner of my blanket, then sat on the bed and flicked through pages of snowball fights and back garden camp-outs, rope swings not strong enough to take your weight and camp-fires that got out of control. Other pages of daring orchard raids and building site trespasses. And scribbled accounts of stone fights with rival gangs and bloody head cuts and rides home in nurses' cars. For a moment, scanning those pages, I wondered just how we all managed to get through it unscathed. Then I realized, of course, that we hadn't.

I flipped through all the clean, neat, unused pages to today's page and wrote: *We've got to hang on to Lightning. Whatever it takes.*

CHAPTER SIX

Cal got a job stacking shelves after school at the local Kwik Save. It was the tenth place he had tried. Just lately Cal hadn't been in the running round town for a Good Citizen award. The manager's young son used to go to school with Toby, so maybe that's what swung it.

Apart from the god-awful twilight zone timewarp called Hadrian's Academy, where every hour seems like a day, the time leading up to the auction seemed to go quickly. Maybe it was because we were all so busy. Tyler said he was working on something he could sell and spent a lot of time sloping off or turning up late all grubby with paint and grease. Kelly collected a load of stuff her gran no longer wanted, and together with things we'd donated, took it to the Sunday boot sale at the church.

Ben and I set up a carwash outside Allonby
Hardware Store every weekday between five
and six-thirty. Old Mr Cottle, who owned the
store, let us fill our buckets from a tap in his
yard and gave us free Turtlewax shampoo in
exchange for keeping his car washed and his
store windows cleaned. Kelly painted us a
sign, saying "Lightning Carwash", in bold red
letters above a gleaming red sportscar. By
around day three, the Lightning Carwashers
were getting such a good reputation that there
were often queues – with those waiting in line
stopping to browse and buy from Mr Cottle's
shop.

The money began to mount. Kelly's boot-
sale was a big help. Someone paid twenty
pounds for one of her gran's items alone; a
little porcelain figure of a boy with a fishing
rod and a little jamjar ready for his first catch.

Everything was going fine, until a week
before the Sunday sale.

Then our world fell apart.

Eight o'clock. We were in the Barn. It was
dark outside. A wind colder than October was
gusting over the Wilderness, creaking the door
and making the window rattle. I was squatting
in the corner talking Tyler through some
maths homework he'd been given. Ben and
Kelly were at the table, hunched over the big
old book of town, talking about the house
down river and what was supposed to have

happened there. Cal was sitting on the edge of the platform, repairing an old clock for one of the women on the Kwik-Save checkouts.

Because the door had been creaking all night, we didn't notice it open. This time there was no warning. And tonight there were not four but six of them standing there when I looked up from the maths book. Corman, Winters, Singer, the new kid, plus two Neanderthals I hadn't seen before. I figured Corman must have brought them along as a precaution after what had happened between him and Cal in the lane. Corman was glowering at me but he didn't move. None of them did. Not yet. The eighty-eight pounds we'd collected so far was only thirty centimetres away from him, hidden behind a loose brick in the wall. We stored our most valuable things there. It wouldn't be the first place they would look, but with six people scouring the Barn, they might eventually find it. I got up and moved to the edge of the platform where Cal had climbed to his feet.

Corman broke the silence. "Got much money?"

"No," I said.

"Plenty," said Cal, looking directly at Corman.

Corman laughed and began to wander the Barn, looking around without any real interest. He would probably get his gang to do the searching. When he'd done a circuit of the Barn he stopped and looked at the broken brickwork behind which our money was hidden.

"Plenty of money?" he echoed Cal, then turning like Billy the Kid going for his six shooter, he reached into the side pocket of his jeans and a moment later he raised a fat wad of folded notes into the air.

"As much as this?" he grinned.

I looked at Cal. He was staring at the money in Corman's hand, trying to figure out how much was actually there. There appeared to be a lot.

"One hundred and ninety-five pounds," Corman crowed and something hot and unpleasant burst in my stomach. Corman gave us one last scornful look, then, like ghosts, he and the rest were gone before we knew it.

For a long while I stared at the open doorway, wondering if Corman hated everyone or just us in particular. I couldn't understand it. We'd never wronged him in any way. He and Cal were even friends once; when Cal was at that age when who you lived near dictated who you hung around with rather than any sort of personal choice. That was a long time ago. Before the lake. Before I knew Cal. Before Corman almost killed Cal and was quickly moved to another part of town. Maybe Corman really hated Cal. Or maybe, I thought for just one crazy, insane moment, he wanted to be his friend again.

Tyler swore, then a heavy, grey sort of silence fell over the Barn, and every time someone tried to pretend that things were going to be OK, they would catch someone else's eye and the silence that followed as their words trailed off told the truth. For almost an hour we sat there with the knowledge that we'd done our best and it hadn't been good enough. We were soldiers, shell-shocked and battle-weary. I wanted to go home, switch on the TV and forget for a while. But five minutes later I was further from home than ever.

CHAPTER SEVEN

"Are you nuts!"

"What the hell are we doing here?"

A branch as sharp-pointed as a pencil brushed against my face and my cheek began to burn as if I'd been slapped. I felt for blood but could see none on my fingers. It was too dark. Everything was grey on black, with more cloud than not blotting out the moon.

As it leads down to the river, the Wilderness becomes thicker and wilder; even in daylight it's difficult to cross. It's marshy too, though not as bad as the killer swamps further down river. At night, crossing the Wilderness is like cutting through some alien landscape.

Tyler was leading us. It was he who got things moving again. Tyler usually did. (Tyler's dad walked out on him and his brothers when Tyler was six and since then the guys his mum has taken up with have stayed just long enough to clear the fridge of beer and her purse of the bingo winnings she had saved. Tyler had been kicked down too many times not to have developed a philosophy for it.) None of us knew exactly where we were going, but I suppose we were all glad to be following someone – despite our gripes and threats that if any of us stood in one more damn squelchy pothole, there'd be blood on the moon tonight.

Tyler stopped only when the river made it impossible to go any further. He turned at the water's edge and looked with those big, brown, innocent cow eyes at us. It was near to low tide and wet mud shone on both sides of the river like train tracks that stretched into the distance in both directions.

Kelly launched a stone into the river. It broke the still surface of the water with a plop that startled a bird out of the reeds. It might have been a plover except I'm not sure if they hang around when the weather turns cold. Ben would know. Birds are sort of a hobby with him. So, just as Cal would happily spend an afternoon pulling apart some broken-down machine, cleaning it and greasing it and mentally cataloguing its parts so that he could rebuild it even better, Ben would patiently sit hidden among the riverside reeds with an old pair of binoculars making note of each new bird that came along.

By the time you get to our age – and I know that's not very old, but even so – you've pretty much figured out what you're good at and what you're not, what you like and what you don't like. Kelly's into art – sketching things and designing anything from jewellery to house interiors. Last year, when my room was redecorated and I thought the plain walls looked too dull, Kelly came round and painted a wide purple stripe that zigzagged over the walls, across the ceiling and back down to the skirting near the window. Tyler's passion is music and he can sing like an angel – sort of high and sweet, like Michael Jackson when he was a little kid and sang "Rockin' Robin". Me, I like football and swimming and reading. Reading is what I do most these days, so I suppose that's what I like best. In books the outsider can win against the odds and the good can triumph over a greater evil.

I looked along the river in both directions. It seemed black as oil in the darkness. There was nothing else to see here except a cluster of trees, willows I think, leaning towards the surface of the water a few metres to our right.

I glanced at Cal, who was pulling his foot out of a soggy hole, and hoped that there was some point to us being here, because the way the night was going there just might be a murder headline in the local paper tomorrow. With a nod, Tyler gave up the moment of mystery. He turned aside and, squelching into the nearby trees, peeled a gap in the curtain of drooping branches. There was something there between the reeds – something dark, shadowy and solid.

It was the reason Tyler had been missing so often recently. He had found the boat about a week ago, drifting downstream like the *Marie Celeste*, and had dragged it into the reed bank.

"I thought we could patch it up," he told us earnestly, as we wandered back into town. "But I think there's a lot of stuff missing. Do you think we can sell it?"

The fact was, and you could tell this even in the light of a burning match, that you'd have to pay someone to take it away. That's probably why it had been cast adrift in the first place. It was a small boat with an enclosed cabin which looked like it had been added on to it by a bad handyman. Everything worth ripping from the boat had been. It was a shell. A rotten, warped and crumbling shell. All the engine parts had gone. The only moving part was the rudder and that didn't move as well as it should have. The only way the boat would ever move again was if it broke free of the reed bank and continued its drifting course to the sea.

Up to his ankles in cold, wet mud, wind cutting through his thin shirt, Cal saw the hopelessness of the situation, drew in his breath and said, "Maybe we ought to forget about raising any more cash, Ty. The bike wasn't such a big deal anyway."

This, I'm sure was untrue. But what Corman had done in the Barn, producing more money than we had managed to make despite all our efforts, had shaken us all. Cal knew that no matter what happened none of us would throw in the towel first. I think he just said what he thought we wanted to hear.

School next day was a nightmare. I was too tired and disgruntled to toe the line. I'd been awake most of the night thinking about what Cal had said. I knew he had lied. Lightning meant everything to him. I hated to see something else he loved be taken away from him. When my form teacher complained about my late arrival and shoddy appearance (I'd not fastened the tie properly and left the collar of my shirt unbuttoned) he gave me the usual Hadrian's pep talk: how we were a respected part of the community and ought to act in an appropriate manner. I replied, "Screw the community, I don't care any more," – or at least I think I did – because a moment later Mr Jarrett's voice split my head open and made me forget everything else.

I was immediately marched to the head-master's office.

When I got home the temperature was

about twenty below freezing. Mum gave me an angry stare as she angrily chopped vegetables at the sink. I knew something was up, but I didn't say anything.

"I've just had a visit from Mr Bateman."

Mr Bateman was the headmaster of Hadrian's.

"Oh," I said, matter-of-factly. I didn't want to be drawn into an argument right then. I hadn't the energy. I just wanted to curl up in bed and listen to some music – old music; from a different time.

"Is that all you have to say for yourself?"

I sighed. "Mum, you don't know how it was. It was no big deal."

"The bill for Hadrian's Academy is never 'no big deal', Jack. Your father and I work hard to give you this opportunity and you're just wasting it."

"I'm not wasting it," I said loudly.

Mum's reply was twice the volume. "You turn up late. You talk back to your teachers. You fight with the other boys." Her voice was rising and her fingers were clenched white around the knife she'd been using. She never pointed out that despite all of this my grades were constantly within the top ten per cent of the school.

"This isn't a state school, Jack. They don't need a big excuse to drop you."

"Fine," I cried. "Let them. I never wanted to

go there in the first place." *I* was yelling now. "Nobody asked me. NOBODY EVER DOES."

I tugged off my tie, threw it at the kitchen waste bin and stormed out.

It was too early to go to the Barn; everyone else would be having tea. I wandered around town, unable to avoid places Cal, Toby and I had been. It was impossible. Our footprints were everywhere.

The fox was there when I got to the Barn and I was glad to see him. I opened him a packet of the dog food he liked best and poured it into Rynn's old bowl. Cal turned up early because he had quit his job at the supermarket. Tyler turned up early because he had given the boat up as a dead loss. Kelly brought a cassette player with her, so, rather than talk, we listened to music most of the night. She brought some karaoke sing along tapes too, but not even Tyler felt like singing right then. That we did with a fury, the following night.

I was late for school again next day. It wasn't deliberate. I'd just got to thinking about things, and sometimes when I do that, time seems to whizz by before I know it. Even before I had made it through my form-room door, my tutor stopped me and said, "Go and see the headmaster, right now."

I went slowly, remembering Mum's words

about Hadrian's not being a state school and them not needing an excuse to drop me. On the headmaster's desk was a long brown envelope. It was turned down so that the name and address were hidden, but I could see the pencilled letters "JC" in the corner. My initials. I thought about what I would say as Mr Bateman sat there, his half-closed eyes staring at his fingers, formed into a steeple on his chest; that I never really liked it here anyway and that the teachers at the state school were better and fairer. Yes. I decided right then and there to go out with a bang.

"We," he said finally, "meet again."

I stared at him. He lifted his gaze and stared back. The clock on the wall tocked rather than ticked – over and over. Tock, tock, tock, tock...

"Look." I scraped out of my chair and got to my feet. "If you've got something to say, then let's just get it over with. OK? I've got better things to do."

Mr Bateman unlocked his fingers and reached for the letter.

"That is very direct, Mr Crandal." He paused and his eyes narrowed thoughtfully, the way they sometimes did when he spoke unscripted to morning assembly. "You have certain characteristics that will be to your advantage. If they are not misdirected."

He slid the letter across the desk, told me to

take it and go.

I considered going home, or to the Barn – somewhere I felt comfortable. But I couldn't wait. I ripped open the envelope right there in the corridor. There was a folded letter and a yellowish slip of paper. I took them over to the chairs outside the secretary's office and sat. I opened the letter. It read:

Dear Master Crandal,

Thank you for your fine contribution to the Inter-school Write-around. We are pleased to inform you that your entry "The Amulet" has won first prize. As stated in the rules, your school will be receiving the one-thousand-pound cheque shortly, and with this letter your personal prize is enclosed.

I unfolded the yellow slip of paper. It was a cheque for two hundred pounds.

CHAPTER EIGHT

The day of the auction was bright and clear, with a cool breeze and the autumnal smell of wood smoke in the air.

Although Hallowe'en was actually two days later, the Hallowe'en open day was held on the twenty-ninth of October, a Sunday, so as not to disrupt the school and its usual weekday routine. Because the auction itself wasn't going to be held until the close of events and we didn't want to hang around school, we passed the time in the sports centre a couple of blocks away, playing bar-football, eating hot dogs and drinking cup after cup of the centre's sweet frothy coffee.

In the huge school hall, only seven rows of seats were occupied. Most of the visitors had seen enough of the school by four o'clock and had wandered off home. We sat alone in the ninth row, so we would have a clear view of what was going on. Corman, Singer and the new kid were slouched on chairs in the second row from the front. For a while it seemed as if nothing was going to happen, then Tyler's form tutor, Mr Leeming, still damp from the charity apple bob, squelched up to the podium and started things rolling.

A fat lady in a hat full of fruit bought the first item – a filing cabinet which she bagged for fifteen pounds. A stack of junk followed – old cricket bats, basketball hoops, a drawing board, a few painting easels from the art room and the only thing that interested any of us – a guitar from the music room. Tyler took a shine to that. I wished I could have bought it for him, but I had to wait until Lightning came up. There was still a chance of being outbid, even by Corman. I was even beginning to feel guilty about buying all that frothy coffee. I wished Lightning would come up soon. Three ancient-looking typewriters brought us to item forty-two; "As seen in the upper school workshop," said Mr Leeming.

Lightning.

Bidding started at fifty pounds and at the time it seemed as if everyone in the hall was interested. As nominated bidder, simply because I'd seen an auction on some farming programme once, I raised my hand each time I thought I should.

Lightning turned out to be the most

expensive item in the sale and the bidding seemed to take for ever. But after a while most dropped out and it was down to me, Corman and a grey-haired guy who wore a cool leather jacket that would have been more suited to his grandson. He dropped out at one hundred and twenty pounds.

Corman bid one forty.

I went one sixty.

The new kid and Singer looked back at us, and whispered something.

One eighty, Corman raised his hand.

Two hundred – me.

Now Corman had turned, frowning.

There was a pause. A long pause. Then Corman called, "Two hundred and twenty-five pounds."

I looked at my friends. Cal leaned over to me and whispered, "It's too much, Jack. Even for Lightning. Don't bid any more."

Corman, Singer and the new kid were all looking back at us now. It was the first time I saw something other than hatred in Corman's eyes. I think it was panic.

It was all over five minutes later. In that short time I had ignored Cal's advice, spent more money than I had ever done in my life, and written myself to the top of Corman's hate list.

Corman and his friends left quickly. Mr Leeming climbed down from the stage and wandered up to us and said, "I know she's a fine motor cycle, but I'm not sure if she's worth that much."

"Yeah," Cal sighed. "That's what I said."

"Will you take her tonight?"

I looked at Cal. He thought for a moment then shook his head. "It still needs work and all the good tools are in the workshop. I think I'll leave it here a while."

When I got home that night I tidied my room and did most of the other jobs I'd been putting off for almost a year, and even after hearing the news that Mum had decided to get involved with the Hadrian's Parent/Teacher Association, I went to bed feeling happier than I had in a long time.

Kelly and Tyler called at my house next morning. It was just after seven o'clock and I was still in bed. I staggered downstairs in slippers and dressing-gown, too sleepy to successfully hide the Winnie the Pooh emblem that waved at you from the pocket. It was a very old dressing-gown that had a lot of sentimental value. I'd have to explain that later, I thought. Then my eyes focused on my friends and I forgot all about that. I knew immediately that something was wrong. Both Kelly and Tyler looked different.

"What's up?" I asked in a thick, early morning voice.

"Something happened last night."

I looked from them to Mum, who, sensing this was private business, picked up her purse from the table and quietly left the room.

"Sit down and we'll tell you."

I sat down. They told me.

Basically, the workshop caught fire. Dobson, the school caretaker, who'd been working later than usual to clear up after the open day, saw smoke puffing out from under the workshop door.

"He tried to tackle the blaze," said Kelly. "And they say he was badly hurt. I heard a huge drum of lubricating oil exploded in the heat of the fire."

I asked just one question. "Does Cal know?"

Tyler said, "No."

As soon as I'd dressed we collected Cal, and raced to the school.

"How bad is it?" Cal asked, trying not to sound anxious.

Five minutes later he had his answer.

The workshop looked like a smoke-blackened cave. Everything that wasn't metal had burned away. The wooden benches lay in little black piles, like sooty volcanic islands. Cal ran straight to where Lightning had been. The bike was lying amid the shattered window glass like a cremated skeleton of some prehistoric creature. The leather seat and rubber tyres had gone. The frame had buckled in the heat. It was hard to believe that this sad sight had ever been Lightning at all.

Only Cal knew that it hadn't.

Cal was halfway through the school gates before I caught up to him.

"What, Cal. What is it?"

"That's not it."

"What?"

"That's a Yamaha frame. Somebody switched bikes."

"Wait!" I cried, trying to catch up and work out what he had said at the same time. "Where are you going?"

If Cal answered me, he had moved too far ahead for me to hear.

Normally, Valley Drive would have been about ten minutes from school, but this time we made it in five. Corman's house was empty. There was no sign of the bike in the garage. Only an old Cortina. You could see in through a side window.

"He's got it. He's got it hidden somewhere." Cal spat as he spun on his heels and started fast down the street.

The coffee bar, where Corman and his gang often hung out before deciding whether to go to or skip school, was round the corner from Tiltson's bike shop. It was beginning to fill with kids when we got there. Kids playing new video games or old pinball, or just standing, talking. Cal pushed through them all, as if they didn't exist, in his hurry to get to the corner table.

Joey Winters and the new kid looked up, startled.

"Where is he?" growled Cal.

After glancing at the new kid, Winters said, "We ... don't know." It sounded to me like a rehearsed reply.

"He took my bike. I want it back."

"It's just a bike," shrugged Winters.

Winters outweighed Cal by about half as much again, but Cal reached over the table and dragged the kid out of his seat. "It was more than just a bike. It was MY bike. THEY CAN'T TAKE THAT AWAY FROM ME TOO!"

Others in the bar looked round. Cal, unaware of the attention, released Winters and sank into the seat opposite the new kid. "I need to know where my bike is."

Cal lifted his head and caught the new kid's eye. Quickly, the kid grabbed his empty glass and returned it to the bar.

"Where's Singer?" I asked Winters and I got the same dumb reply.

"We ... don't know."

The new kid knocked against me when he returned with a fresh glass of cola. Some of it spilt over my school blazer and splashed on to the table, spraying over Cal, who, staring down at the table, didn't appear to notice.

"Sorry," said the kid without thinking and Winters looked at him curiously, as if he'd spoken some strange piece of Chinese.

The kid shuffled uncomfortably. He looked at me and frowned. "Look, we don't know where the bike is, OK? Corman went riding pillion with Richy last night. They were going to the Oakley beer festival – they're probably sleeping it off in a roadside ditch somewhere."

Corman did return, riding on the back of Richy Singer's dirt-bike. They were stopped heading into town by the police because of the bike's faulty exhaust. It spat out thick black soot and sounded like a submachine-gun.

It wasn't designed for road use.

I got to Hadrian's in time for second period maths. Cal made me go and to be honest, I was glad to be there. It was good to have nothing but a dizzying algebra problem to think about. At lunch I decided not to sit alone. I wanted to talk about something – anything but bikes. Peter Cartwright was sitting on his own at the far table. He was OK. Not one of the silver spoon boys. Boys who think they're special just because of their parents' status.

"You don't like motor bikes, do you?" I asked before I had even sat down.

"No," he said. "I like horses. Horses are great. Better than bikes, better than people."

Horses. Thank God.

I'd never spoken much to Peter before. I guess I'd written him off as just one of the others. Today I found out he had a horse called Hunter, and I realized that Hunter meant as much to Peter as Lightning did to Cal.

"Do you have any pets?" he asked me.

I thought about the fox, then shook my head and said no.

I scooped a forkful of tuna pasta into my mouth and crazy though it was, probably the trauma doing something to my brain, I began to think that Hadrian's really wasn't so bad after all.

Peter stood and said, "I'm going to the vending machine. You want a drink of something?"

"Yeah, OK." I nodded, reaching into my outside blazer pocket for change. I pulled a twenty and a fifty-pence piece, and something else. A little sachet of sugar. It was the kind of thing you get at the sports centre when you order frothy coffee. But I'd never worn my school blazer to a place like that. I wouldn't wear it at all if it were up to me. Then I remembered the coffee bar this morning and turned the sachet over in my fingers. There was dark, uneven writing over the faint blue brand name. It said, simply: "GHOST HOUSE".

* * *

There was some sort of protest rally going on in the next town and a lot of our regular police had been drafted in as back-up. The few that remained didn't have much time to listen to us. I got Cal out of school and told him what I thought: that the new kid had slipped the sugar packet into my pocket at the coffee bar and tipped me off that Corman and Singer had rode their bikes cross-country to the Halloway House. They had hidden Lightning there and returned on Singer's dirt-bike, same day. The Ghost House. The bike was in the Ghost House. Could you think of a better place to hide something?

The weary desk sergeant was not impressed. He said that only a TV detective with more money than sense would waste his time on such flimsy evidence. It was no use trying to argue. In line behind us was a scruffy old guy, clinging tight to a cider bottle while singing "Love Me Tender". Before we left, the sergeant assured us that someone would have a quiet word with Corman, just to confirm his where-abouts.

"Just a waste of time," Cal spat as we pushed our way out. Without another word his fast walk turned into a run.

"Where are you going?" I called after him. I could never keep pace with Cal over any

distance greater than a hundred metres. I
didn't even try.

"I'm gonna get Lightning back myself!"

For the second time that day I had to endure
the frowns, smirks and rude noises my
Hadrian's uniform was getting from the un-
uniformed kids at the town comprehensive. It
was afternoon change-round and the place
was bustling. I thought I would never spot
anyone in the crowds, then almost immediately I saw Kelly among five or six other girls
in the doorway across the playground. She
was no taller than the rest, but somehow she
seemed to stand out. She was certainly the
prettiest. It's strange I know, but having
known Kelly since we were kids, I hadn't
noticed that before. It's only lately that it had
become more and more obvious.

Kelly suggested that Tyler and Ben would be
round the back of the school, playing football
with the rest of their class. She was partly
right. Ben was playing. Tyler and another kid
were trying to shin up each side of the nearest
goalpost. I think it was a race to reach the
crossbar.

When we were together I told them what
happened.

"The bike's at the *Halloway House*?" Tyler
said with awe.

"And Cal's on his way to get it?" Kelly asked.

I nodded.

"But how?" said Ben. "I thought you said the land was too marshy to cross on foot."

"It is. You have to ride round it in a big, curving detour."

Tyler was about to cut in and tell me that since Lightning had gone, he didn't have a bike to ride around that curve. But I stopped him and added, "Unless you go by river and sail right through the marshland."

"In that wreck we saw on the riverbank, you mean?" asked Kelly, surprised.

"It's not that bad," said Tyler. "I've been doing some work on it."

"Could Cal do that? Would he do that, alone?"

I shrugged. The way Cal had been acting lately I figured there was nothing he wouldn't do. I was worried. My mum once told me, after I had my mountain bike stolen from outside the newsagents, that people aren't born bad; things happen. They change. I was worried that Cal was changing; growing up too fast, growing away, growing to be like Corman. I didn't really know Corman when he was younger. I only know what Cal has told me. He and Corman were friends before I knew Cal. Little kid, neighbour-type friends. Birthday party stuff. Cal, Corman and his cousins, twins a little younger than Cal, sometimes played together. Cal told me once, after

Corman's first trespass into our Barn when the other Barnstormers had left us to wander into town alone, about the last time they ever played together. It was a Sunday. Cal, Corman and the cousins, Chris and Mikey, had been playing commandos. They'd started early, using guns made from scrap wood with nailed-on handgrips where rifle-grips ought to have been. Corman's garden, eight down from Cal's, was base camp. Cal's garden was the weapons store. Between these two positions mines were hidden so that you had to balance on fences(Mikey's speciality), climb over dustbins and crawl over cars, always aware that enemy snipers were watching from the woods. Before lunch they had collected the ammo and won the war and returned to base camp for rations. Polos and liquorice and Smarties. Not much for ravenous, battle-weary soldiers. The twins wanted more. Corman, their leader, said his mum kept a bottle of special rations inside the house. Like the Smartie power pills only better and brighter. Special marching pills. Cal was happily following Corman and the twins for his share of the ration when his own leader called to him from home. This was when Cal was still little Andrew Calahan, a time when, if his mum shouted at him to come in and clean up for lunch, he did so, running.

Corman and the twins silently crept up to the bathroom and spent the time before their meal, not cleaning up but popping the bright coloured pills from the forbidden cabinet. Corman woke up almost a week later in Hartford General Hospital. The twins never did.

CHAPTER NINE

At around the time we should all have been returning home with our school books, ready to wash all that horrible education out of our heads with a good half-hour of *Wacky Races* or *Scooby Doo*, we had been walking along the riverside for about half an hour and things were beginning to look unfamiliar. We had passed the last recognizable landmark, Oakley Church, a mile or so back. The plants along the riverbank were wilder here, in places you had to hack your way through. But if you veered away from the river and its plant life you ended up knee-deep in peat bog.

The river in autumn isn't blue, it's silvery-grey. On days when the water is moving slowly it looks like a great long glistening snail-track. This was how the river looked now; and the faint ground mist that edged the bank made the river seem almost solid. Only the occasional splash of a kingfisher or dipper, or a stone found and lobbed by one of us told the truth. Tyler tried to skim a flat stone over the surface but it sank without trace. It was something he could never do. He tried; every time a flat stone came his way he gave it his best shot, never gave up, but never quite got it right. Even Toby tried to teach him how to do it, but all that happened was that Tyler got so mad at getting it wrong so often; during one especially angry throw he lost his balance and ended up face down in the low tide sludge.

As it reaches our town, the river is well into its mature stage. If you've ever done this subject in geography you'll know that it's slower and wider than it is at its earlier, youthful phase. And because it's flowing more slowly it doesn't cut a fast, straight line through the land, but bends with it instead. So as we were walking along the bank it was only possible to see a short way ahead before the river curved again and disappeared behind another thick growth of hawthorn and reed-mace. There was no sign of the boat on the next curve.

"We're gonna get lost," ranted Tyler. "We're gonna get lost and die of starvation."

Kelly pointed at the water and assured him that as long as the river remained just a few feet away, the chances of getting lost were pretty slim. All we had to do was follow it back.

"Oh, yeah." Tyler grinned stupidly, then began hacking at the plants with new vigour.

The further we travelled, the slower we got, and with every new clump of trees we approached, met and then passed, the terrible maybes grew in my mind.

Maybe Cal was miles away.

Maybe he was back home wondering where the heck everyone had got to.

Maybe the boat had simply drifted free of the reed bed days ago.

Maybe it had sunk.

But maybe ... just maybe ... the boat was behind the next cluster of leaning trees.

Or the next...

Or the next...

Or maybe the next...

It was like playing a slot machine. With every coin you put in, the chances of hitting the jackpot seemed better. But today there was no jackpot. No ringing bells. No sign of Cal. Nothing except more and more maybes.

Maybe we should turn back. Cut our losses. We'd done our best. Maybe now it was time to let the adults take over. Perhaps they could handle it better.

The weary look on Ben's face said, Yeah. OK.

The sigh Kelly couldn't quite hold in said, Maybe so.

But then there was always the next bend.

So we carried on.

The smell of wood smoke drifted over from a nearby smallholding. It reminded me of November bonfires, toffee apples and potatoes baked black in their skins. It reminded me that it was round about tea-time.

"Red sky at night," murmured Ben.

There was a coloured tinge behind the broken grey clouds now. It would be dark soon. Dusk had crept upon us.

Dusk changes the rules, makes everything different; not just in the way the shadows lengthen and make, for that short period before true darkness falls, everything clearer – sharper. But it changes the way you feel, too. As darkness begins to fall, all the wide open spaces in which you go your separate ways disappear and you draw together, maybe for warmth, maybe for safety, or perhaps just for plain old comfort.

"I'm starving," moaned Tyler.

"Don't be such a loser, Tubs."

Tyler looked at me and yelled, "AM-BU-LANCE!" at the top of his voice. A pair of grouse, hiding in the long grass close to where we were walking, flapped up in wild panic.

Tyler spun round fast. Kelly and I followed a fraction later. Ben, not knowing what was going on, stopped and gawped. I grabbed my collar. Tyler and Kelly grabbed theirs. Then we squatted fast to the ground.

When we'd finished Ben looked at us as if we'd all lost our minds.

"What the hell was all that about?"

Kelly tipped me a wink.

Like a lot of things that happened when we were kids, I don't exactly remember how it began, but it goes something like this: years ago there was an old woman who worked down-town and was so wrinkled and warty that we were sure she was a witch, and she told us one day that whenever an ambulance drives across your path, you had to touch your collar and say a prayer. I guess when you're nine years old you believe that stuff. But we knew no prayers except our favourite "For What We Are About to Receive", so instead we invented this crazy rap routine which went:

Hold your collar. Never swall–ar.
Turn around. And touch the ground.

Everybody chanted it except Tyler, who became a human beat-box to the rap. Weird, I know. But we were only little kids. A pretty weird bunch of kids at that.

"You've got to say it," Tyler told Ben, "whenever an ambulance passes – otherwise you're dead meat. This old lady told us."

"So where is this old lady now?"

"Dead," said Tyler. "She forgot to hold her collar. She was a witch. She taught me stuff.

103

Taught me how to find water with a Y-shaped twig."

Tyler snapped off a branch from one of the bushes. "You hold the snapped-off branch at the tops of the Y and when it comes near to water, the point is drawn mysteriously towards it."

My feet were beginning to ache. Heavy brogues are part of the Hadrian's winter uniform and they have hard leather soles. I was developing a blister. We had come another mile or so, there was still no sign of Cal, and the maybes were back with a vengeance. Then suddenly, like a dog spotting a cat, or maybe only sensing it, Tyler stiffened and ran forwards several paces.

"There he is!" he pointed. "There's the boat."

I looked but could see nothing but a tiny grey smudge on the riverbank a mile away. In the growing dimness it could have been anything. A dead tree. A riverside shack. From this distance it was hard to tell if it was even in or out of the water.

But the thing is, if the Barnstormers wanted the answer to something like a sticky maths problem they'd been set for homework, they'd come to me. But when the questions were less mathematical, odd questions like – was that hole dug by a rabbit or a badger, or, is the smell drifting over from the school canteen apple pie or lemon meringue, or, what's the name of the park keeper's dog? – they usually called on Tyler. Tyler with his keen nose, keen ear, keen memory, keen eye.

"It's a shack," I suggested as we got nearer and began to see more clearly.

"It's the boat," insisted Tyler.

"It's nothing like the boat. It's not even in the water."

"It's the boat!"

"It's not!"

It was the boat.

But I was right about something. The boat wasn't in the water. It was beached on the riverbank – stuck.

When we reached the boat we found Cal among the reeds on the riverbank, almost knee-deep in mud, trying to push the boat back into the water. He hadn't noticed us coming. He'd been too caught up in his task. He was breathless and sweat had matted his hair to his forehead. It looked as if he had been struggling to get the boat back in the water for some time. As we neared the boat Tyler pulled a little mouth organ from his jeans back pocket and disappeared behind one of the trees. Then, after blowing a two-tone police siren into his mouth organ, he called through cupped hands, "This is the police. We have you surrounded. Turn around and come out of the water with your hands on your head. One false move and we start a-shootin'.'"

I pushed past Tyler as he started his "You have the right to remain silent" bit, and jumped down from the grass bank near to where the boat was stuck. Bad move. In an instant my feet said goodbye to terra firma, as cold wet mud oozed up over my shins. I swore – to cover up my foolishness as much as any-thing else – and with a loud slurp I pulled up my left foot. It was caked with tarry mud and felt as heavy as a weighted diver's boot. I won-dered what my teacher would say if he could see me now. (Last term he almost coughed up a lung because I turned up for class with a shoelace missing. I tried to explain that the lace had snapped, but it was like trying to ask an alarm clock to stop ringing. "No laces! No laces! NO LACES!!!"

If he could now see me he would have a stroke: *Black laces!!! Muddy shoes!!! Soggy socks!!!*)

Cal was looking at us with surprise.

"I think I just got myself a year's detention," I said.

As Ben and Kelly came up, Cal wiped the back of his hand over his forehead, streaking it with dirt and sweat.

"That uniform was never going to win you any prizes," drawled Cal. "Except maybe twit of the week."

I grinned in spite of myself. Ever since my

parents sent me to Hadrian's, Cal had hated the idea of its uniform and its rules and its attitude, and he took every chance to take a cheap shot.

I lifted a clump of mud from my heel and launched it in Cal's direction. It hit home just below his chin and spattered across his neck.

"You don't exactly look like Joe Cool yourself." I laughed but before I could say another word, Cal lunged for me. I managed to keep my balance for half a second and then found myself falling back against the slope of the riverbank. Before I knew it, I was pinned down, helpless.

"Say 'Submit'."

"No," I gasped, trying to shake off Cal and break free.

"Say it!" Cal shifted his balance so he could pin me down better.

"No!"

Cal reached for the dark mud I'd spattered across his face and began to run a finger of it from my forehead down my nose like Indian warpaint.

"Say it, now."

I struggled again but had no luck.

Another line of warpaint – this one a diagonal stripe across my cheek.

"Come on Jack-o," Tyler called. "You can fight him."

I tried to push free but Cal shifted his weight

until his elbow was digging into the hollow above my collarbone, and from then on the more I struggled, the more painful it got. During all the years I'd known Cal, through all the fun fights and tussles we'd had, he had learned exactly how to use his strength against me. I gave one last push in an attempt to shake him just enough to allow me to worm out of his hold, but as usual Cal saw it coming and countered with a painful twist of the arm.

"OK. OK. I submit, you big stupid jerk, all right?"

Cal relaxed his hold enough for me to roll free. I looked at my school uniform and decided not even to attempt to brush the dirt away. There was just too much. In my pockets, in my hair, on my back, across my face.

"Oh, look," I heard Kelly say from the safety of the riverbank. "It's Tonto and the Lone Ranger."

"What's up, Cal. You stuck or something?"

"Yes, Tyler. I'm stuck in the mud."

"Where're you going?"

"I'm not going anywhere at the moment. You want to give me a push off?"

Without a word or a thought for his own clothes, Ben jumped down into the mud. He still felt, at least as far as Cal was concerned, I think, that he wasn't quite one of the gang – but then maybe none of us were Barnstormers any more. When Toby died I think that old gang died with him.

Ben waded out to the boat and began to pull.

Cal looked at him and nodded. "Thanks."

Following Ben's lead, Tyler and Kelly jumped down into the mud, and as we all sloshed to the boat and readied for the big push, I repeated the question Tyler had asked. But with one difference. "Where're *we* going?"

"We?"

"Yeah." Kelly looked at me and then nodded. "We."

"Down river," Cal replied slowly.

"Where?" asked Tyler. "To Donnovan's Reach?"

"No, further."

"France?" said Tyler. "The West Indies?"

"I think we all know where we're going," I said.

"The Halloway House," Tyler hissed in his best spooky voice.

"In this thing?" I slapped the hull of the boat. It sounded hollow – useless – dead.

Cal replied with a nod.

CHAPTER TEN

After two false starts and a couple of mud slides we got the boat into the water and floating. The tiller, the arm that controlled the direction of the boat, was at the back, so Cal kept with it, steering as best he could. Kelly and I stayed on deck, Kelly using as an oar the thin plank of wood Cal had brought along, while Ben and Tyler went below to investigate.

Almost immediately there was a shriek: Ben's not Tyler's. And a moment later, from down below, sprang the fox. I had to improvise a rugby dive and grab it before it belly-flopped into the water.

"You brought the fox along?"

"Ship's mascot." Cal shrugged a little self-consciously. The old Cal.

I hooked an arm around the fox and scratched its ear (something that since it had got to know us, it seemed to enjoy) and looked around the boat. Tyler had filled in the cracks that had been so obvious the last time I'd seen the boat, with wood filler and varnish, and had even given the deck a coat of thick white gloss remarkably similar to the stuff they'd been using on the sports refurbishments.

Cal noticed me giving the boat the once-over and shrugged. "It's not exactly the *QE2* but at least it floats."

"She's a good ship," said Tyler defensively.

"She's better with an engine," I said and then looked at Cal.

"Any supplies?"

"Sorry, Jack. I didn't have time."

"But I'm starving."

"I wasn't expecting stowaways."

"Have we passed Raven's Reach?"

"No," Cal answered, then asked Tyler why he wanted to know.

"We could call into Ravensworth. Get some stuff. You know. Provisions. We could make sandwiches. I've got a knife to cut the bread."

I'm not sure if this, coming from Tyler, could have been officially classed as a brain-wave, or whether it was just hunger clouding my judgement. But right then, if I'd been the Wizard of Oz and I'd had a diploma to spare, I'd have given it to him gladly.

By the time we got to the Reach, only about half an hour later, all daylight had gone from the sky, but the moon had risen, round and bright, and lit a silvery path along the river. We drifted the boat a little way further downstream and tied it up among a clump of leaning willow trees. This to me seemed cautious enough, but Tyler wouldn't leave until we had all but smothered the boat in a blanket of leafy camouflage. I only hoped we could find it again.

Ravensworth was a small place, halfway between a town and a village. None of us had been there before, but Kelly, because her gran could tell you almost anything about the area (and probably over the years, had) suggested that there would be plenty of places in Ravensworth to buy supplies. And we'd be able to phone home with some story about why we wouldn't be coming back tonight. The route we took – a narrow lane hedged between fields, one ploughed, the other ripe with some sort of root crop – turned out to be longer than we'd expected, probably two miles or so. Every few minutes Tyler would glance into the darkness behind us, muttering things like, "You think the boat's OK? Did we hide it well enough? Maybe someone'll find it and tow it away?"

I said I didn't think we could be so lucky.

Tyler told me, in his own colourful way, to shut up.

Kelly assured him that we had thrown so

many branches and reeds over the boat the chances were that not even we would be able to find it. So Tyler forgot about the boat and started carping on about the fox instead. He hoped it would be all right. We'd left it dozing in the cabin. What if something happened? Could foxes swim?

The lane led down on to a small patch of wasteland and beyond that to the back of the half-filled, brightly-lit car park of a small Gateway supermarket. As we passed them, a family loading what looked like a year's supply of groceries into the back of a big estate car, caught sight of us and gaped as if they'd just glimpsed something out of a late night horror movie. I'd forgotten that Cal and I were caked almost head to toe in drying mud and, even worse, when I spotted my reflection in the car's tinted windows I saw the warpaint smudges across my face. I tried to rub them off without much success. Kelly dipped her handkerchief in a nearby puddle and smoothed it over my brow. "That's better," she whispered with breath that smelt as sweet as summer. "I knew there was a cute kid in there somewhere."

A cute kid!

Tyler slapped my back. "Well, I wouldn't go so far as that, but at least now we won't have to chain him up outside."

"Listen, Greg," I pulled Tyler to one side

before we went in to the store. "Don't touch anything, OK?"

"What do you mean, '*touch*'?"

"Steal. Just leave things alone. We've got enough problems without having to bail you out for shoplifting, right?"

Tyler narrowed his eyes at me, then shrugged and muttered something I could only guess was OK. I hated the resentful look he had given me, but I had to keep a close check on him. Sometimes Tyler did crazy things to impress Cal, not knowing that Cal was far too smart to be wowed by something as stupid as shoplifting.

The store was almost empty, with only a few evening shoppers strolling along the narrow aisles between the tall shelves. We had pooled what money we had – Cal pitching in the biggest sum – and that was enough to buy a two litre bottle of ginger ale (the only drink we could all agree on), bags of nuts and crisps, and peanut butter, bananas and bread, together with a large block of chocolate which Ben said was good for energy. He used to be in the Scouts and knew what were the right things to take on an expedition. "They take it up mountains and stuff," he said.

We didn't spend all the money – I'd kept a handful of coins for emergencies and so that we could phone home and let everyone know that we wouldn't be back tonight.

At the checkout, Kelly paid for the groceries and began talking to the girl who had taken our money. The girl had stopped to admire the enamel brooch Kelly was wearing and wanted to know where she might buy one. I knew that Kelly had made the brooch herself and smiled with pride as I began bagging our supplies. I had just picked up the last packet of crisps when an alarm bell in my head sounded as I heard, "Hey, put those back, you little thie..."

After that I didn't hear any more. I just grabbed the bag and like the others ahead of me, I ran.

Suddenly the street, which only minutes ago had been almost deserted, seemed to be crawling with people; old women who had to be dodged, little kids who had to be shoved, shaggy dogs that had to be leapt over.

We finally stopped running after ducking into a shadowy alley awash with the faint, twangy sound of country and western music. It was only then, as we caught our breath in damp air that smelled of stale beer, that we noticed that one of us was missing. Cal hadn't made it. I remembered him bolting for the side exit as we ran for the main front entrance. There must have been a security guard on the side door.

About five times more slowly than the way we had raced away from the supermarket, we shambled back towards it. The street seemed much quieter now that there was no hurry to escape.

"What happened?" I asked, feeling a little drunk from running so fast.

"It was Cal," said Ben. "That lady shouted at Cal."

"He must have nicked something." Tyler jabbed a finger in my direction. "You tell me not to steal anything and Cal goes and does it instead."

The silence that followed was broken by Kelly, saying something I would have been quick to say not so long ago. "Cal wouldn't do that. He's not that stupid."

"Maybe he is," I said. "I mean, he has done some pretty stupid things lately. It's…"

I stopped as a smart young couple, laden with shopping, edged carefully past us as if we were some half-tamed creatures that couldn't quite be trusted. When they had passed, Kelly hooked an arm around my shoulder and started us walking again.

"It's worrying, I know," she said softly – to me alone rather than to us all – "but you can't pin him down, Jack. That's what his parents are trying to do, and the more they push him, the harder he fights it."

"So what do we do?"

"Firstly," Kelly said calmly, "we've got to get him out of that supermarket."

* * *

117

The store, as we peered through the window wondering what to do next, was almost empty. Spying between posters for dog meat and detergent I could see only two shoppers – a fat man dipping into one of the freezers at the back of the shop, like a walrus diving into an arctic ice hole, and an old lady chatting to the girl behind the cigarette counter near the entrance. After what seemed like an eternity of blankness I looked again at the cigarette counter, then pulled a handful of coins from the pocket of my blazer and wandered into the shop. The old lady bought a packet of menthol cigarettes and a *People's Friend Weekly*. The fat man, who had followed her to the counter, bought a puzzle magazine. When he had left I strode up to the counter and said, "Ten Number Six, please." I'd heard Cal say this at similar kiosks. The girl, pretty I suppose, but no threat to Kelly, took my coins and dropped them into the cash register. As she was handing me the cigarettes and the change, I smiled and said, as casually as I could, "I hear you just had some trouble?"

"Just another shoplifter." She twirled her hair through the fingers of her left hand. "We get them all the time. It's no big deal."

"Did he get away?"

Tipping her head towards a tall, thin uniformed man with pale skin and a black moustache about six sizes too big, she said,

"Nobody gets away from Carver. The kid's banged up in the old storeroom out the back. Waiting for the police to come."

The alley at the back of the supermarket was long and narrow with high walls of smooth brick. Standing in that alley was like being at the bottom of a long deep trench; like one of the trenches in the battlefields of the First World War.

Being the best climber, I scaled the wall so I could look down into the floodlit yard below. It was mostly open space. There was a rusty yellow forklift truck in one corner that looked like it hadn't moved in years. Beside it was a stack of milk bottle crates and two waste bins. The large ones on wheels that they have in schools. At Greyland Comprehensive they're always being set on fire. There was a green door at the far right of the building, but it had no exterior handle. A fire exit, I figured. One you could only open from the inside. Spread evenly across the wall to the left of the door were four windows. All were frosted glass. Three were about a metre square, almost head height. The fourth window was long and narrow, set higher up the wall.

"What's there?" Ben called anxiously from below.

"A way in," I answered.

One of the square windows, the one nearest the waste bins and a sign saying: "Restricted

Area – Deliveries to Side Entrance", was open a crack. Without allowing myself time to think about what I was doing, I dropped quietly into the yard and started for the window. I wondered, too late to do anything about it, if there was a security guard patrolling the grounds. A guard with a dog. A big, drooling Alsatian with a jaw full of razor-sharp teeth. But I made it to the window without shouts or barks, so I figured there wasn't. It wasn't the window to the old storeroom. I realized this when my right foot, in its Hadrian's uniform brogue, sloshed into a toilet bowl and I felt chilly water seep into my sock. I swore under my breath, and had barely lifted my foot from the bowl and glanced around the small cubicle when, somewhere ahead of it, a door opened and two *women* entered and began doing something at the sinks with running water and clinking bottles, while talking about someone called Nick and a place in town that served brilliant banana fritters. They left only when someone shoved their head around the door and called, "Shell, you're wanted on pricing. The bleeper's blown a fuse again."

I'm glad to say the corridor was empty when I cracked open the door and peered cautiously out. There's really no way of sneaking out of a ladies' toilet without feeling guilty, even if you did get there by mistake. It's a little like passing through the ladies underwear section of a department store to get to the sports gear on the other side. You hurry on through with your head down hoping that nobody spots you on the way. I shot out of the toilet while the coast was clear and hurried along the long, narrow corridor that looked odd in the blinking light of a faulty neon bar. Most of the doors were labelled, but none with the sign I was looking for. The old storeroom, if it was here at all, must have been behind one of the two unmarked doors. Looking more closely I saw that only one of the doors had a key in the lock, in fact only one of them had a keyhole, so I figured that this was the door behind which Cal was being held.

Aware of the fact that I had no good explanation for being where I was, I turned the key, grasped the handle and shoved open the door.

It was a small room, dim and dusty and, but for a few wooden crates and some unused dexion shelving, empty. Could the cops have got there already and dragged their catch off to the station? I crept in, wondering what Andrew Calahan would look like in one of those front and side photographs they take of criminals, when I spotted the long, narrow, high-mounted window I'd seen from outside. I also noticed that someone had dragged one of the empty shelf units over to the window and tilted it against the wall, like a stepladder. I followed the scrape marks along the floor

121

and touched the shelf. Cold metal. It felt just about strong enough to support me. Hoping I was right, I put my damp school brogue on the first shelf step and was about to push up when I heard, firstly voices, then a moment later, the key rattling behind me. Somebody was trying to unlock the door I had already locked. I scrambled for the crates in the corner and quickly ducked down as the door swung open.

"I'm sure I locked it. Could have sworn I did, Constable," said a woman's voice. Then she let out a strange sort of gargling sound, as if someone had dropped a cold key down the back of her blouse, and said, "The window!"

Two sets of footsteps clopped across the room.

"He's out of it." I heard a man say. "Jumped over those waste bins you've got out there like he's just sat on a wasp's nest."

"I only left him for a minute," muttered the woman. "And he said he wouldn't try anything silly. And he looked such a nice boy too. Messy, but with a sort of sad, noble air about him."

"Well, your noble young lad's just spread his noble young wings and flown it, Mrs Wickham," said the first cop.

"He'll be halfway to the quarry by now," added constable two, stepping, I think, into the centre of the room. It was hard to tell. Crouched tightly behind those small, soapy-smelling crates in the corner, I didn't dare move to see.

"You'd do well to get a good sturdy lock on that window," suggested cop number one. He sounded *big* – like a St Bernard next to his wiry whippet partner, who said, "These kids are definitely getting worse. Bold as you like nowadays."

"Yesterday," began the big one, as cramp began to nip into my leg, "we nabbed a nipper no bigger than this walking out of the Middleton Saver-store with a whopping great radio-cassette player tucked under his arm."

"Shocking," said the woman.

"I'll say," said the whippet and I wished I had some sort of magical fast-forward controller because my cramp had grown teeth and had started to gnaw.

"Oh, not that there's much chance of getting it back now, but for the record what had this one taken?"

"A packet of Polo mints," said the woman.

"A packet of Polos?" said both cops together.

The woman, I guess, nodded and the policemen left shortly after this. A few minutes later, I left too. The way Cal had done: through the window.

Cal, Kelly, Ben and Tyler were waiting for me in the alley.

"What kept you?" said Tyler, sitting with Ben up against the wall.

Used paper from the nearby chip shop blew past us like western tumbleweed. Not far away a car horn blared angrily.

"You run into trouble with the Boys in Blue?" Cal asked, goading me. Making light of something grave was sometimes a way of acknowledging something you'd done without actually saying thanks, and what you did when a friend did this is shrug, and calmly say, "It was no big deal," and to pretend this is true you nonchalantly pick a speck of dirt from the arm of your blazer as if everything was fine.

I went to do this and saw that there was just too much. My school coat was still caked in mud from the riverbank. My foot was still soaking too, from its swim in the ladies toilet, I realized as anger washed over me. I spun round fast and glared at Cal.

"Look, thanks, Jack," he began. "I—"

"*Are you deliberately looking to get us into trouble or are you just plain stupid?*"

"What?" Cal looked suddenly confused.

"*I thought you wanted to find the damn bike. You're hardly going to do that, stuck in some cop station charged with shoplifting.*"

"I didn't lift anything," Cal defended through clenched teeth.

"Except that pocket of Polos," I countered,

nodding towards Tyler. Cal had given them to him and Tyler was popping one into his mouth as we were arguing over them.

"I picked them up. I was looking at them. That's all. Then that old cow shouted at me like I'd done something wrong and I got mad—"

"And then you ran for the exit!"

Ben got to his feet. "It was just a packet of Polos, Jack."

"I can speak for myself," Cal spat.

"You don't even like Polos," I shrieked, not caring about the people passing the entrance to the alley.

"Then why would I steal them?" he shouted his reply.

"I don't know. I don't know why you do anything any more."

"Because it doesn't matter. Nothing matters. Whatever you do, things will happen that you have no control over." His hands were clenched and his voice had dropped to a whisper. "I'm right, aren't I? I'm not crazy. Things happen, don't they?"

"Yes," I said softly. "Things happen. Bad things happen, but *good* things too, sometimes."

"Good things?"

"Yes. I don't mean magic or anything like that. I mean like in doing something good. People doing something good for you, even if on the surface you don't deserve it. Like a teacher you hardly know sticking his neck out and covering for you when you ought to have been punished."

Cal looked at me unsurely.

"Or you doing something good for someone else," I said.

"Like what?"

"Like … like missing the sports centre to make a go-kart for a kid whose skateboard had been stolen."

A thin smile showed on Cal's lips. It was Toby's go-kart and he'd been thrilled with it. All the money in the world couldn't have bought him a better one.

"Like your friends," said Cal, "sailing with you to a haunted house where some maniac murdered his family?"

I nodded because I could think of nothing important to say. Then I put an arm over Cal's shoulder and leaving the others to follow, walked him out of that alley.

"You know what I've been doing?" I said as we made it on to the street.

"What?"

"Standing with my foot in a ladies' toilet bowl."

Cal's laughter at this, though short and a little embarrassed, was worth all the money we'd raised and more.

Kelly, Tyler and Ben caught up to us a

126

moment later and suggested we find a telephone.

"Jack," suggested Tyler, "can phone Dial a Drip." And as we were shambling along the high street to a shape he swore was a public phone box, he offered me one of the hot Polos and said, "Jack-o. When my old grandad dies, can I adopt you as a replacement?"

I did not dignify this with an answer.

The shape Tyler had pointed out *was* a telephone booth. One of the old-style red ones with rectangular windows that they have in old towns to keep them in character. I dropped the money I had left in the coin slot and dialled my number. It rang for almost a minute before I realized that nobody would be home; my dad would be having another late meeting with his accountant friends, Mum would be at her usual badminton class and my brother would be at the swimming pool. I called the sports club and left a message for Mum saying I was helping Ben with his science project and would be staying overnight. Ben's call was pretty much the same, but in reverse. He also asked his mum to call round Tyler's house – which didn't have a telephone – and tell Mrs Tyler that Greg would be staying the night at my place too. Kelly had to be a bit more careful. Although Mr Walshaw liked to joke around with me, Cal and Tyler, if Kelly told him she was spending the night at any of our houses, he would have a fit. Kelly told him that a girl-friend from school had invited her to spend the night at the local stables where she worked at weekends. All Cal said was, "Hi. It's me. Everything's fine. I'll be back tomorrow."

Then, with not so much as a penny between us, we turned back up the high street. As we passed the supermarket, Tyler whacked on the window near to the checkout lady who'd shouted at Cal. As she looked up from counting the day's takings, Tyler pulled one of the Polos from his pocket and popped it, slowly and deliberately, into his mouth. Then we started running again.

CHAPTER ELEVEN

"Are we going the right way?" asked Kelly. For some reason she was looking at me, even though Tyler was leading. We were walking, at least we hoped we were, along the long hedged lane we'd taken coming into town from the river. But things looked different. Changed. We should have headed straight back after phoning home but Ben and Tyler wanted to watch *Cartoon Carnival* through the window of a television rental shop down one of the side streets. It was *Tom and Jerry*. Tyler's favourite. He liked to see the little guy win.

Now cloud had blotted out most of the moon and stars and the wind had whipped up too, whispering through the hedge like night voices. I was beginning to think we had the wrong lane, that we were totally lost. But I didn't say anything. If we were lost, grouching

129

about it wouldn't help us much, and being likened to Tyler's grandfather once in a day is more than enough.

"No more songs?" I said to Tyler. At the start of the lane he had softly crooned out some old rock 'n' roll, most of which I recognized but couldn't name. But one song, a record by Neil Sedaka, I remembered clearly because I'd heard it before and the lyric, about an ordinary girl who had suddenly blossomed into something special, reminded me of Kelly.

"I don't feel like singing any more," Tyler grumbled. "My feet are singing for me." I think we all felt that way. Right then, following that dark, whispery lane to who knows where, our Barn seemed a long way away.

Something flitted overhead. Something dark. A bat, I thought, but couldn't be sure. It was there and then gone too quickly.

The darkness drew our thoughts to the Halloway House.

"You don't really think it's haunted, do you?" said Kelly in a whisper.

I said I doubted it. It was what I wanted to hear someone else say.

We all knew the story of Bill Halloway. It had been passed down from one playground generation to the next for almost thirty years. Bill Halloway was a grave digger, the local misfit, the town drunk, always brawling or poaching, causing disturbances. "It was the voices," he would say when the police finally showed. "They made me do it." They say Bill was always hearing voices. They say that was the reason he gave for leaving town, for marrying the widow who owned the ranger's old house deep in North Castleton Woods, and it was the voices, they say, that caused him late one cold October night to steal through the dark house that now bears his name, and murder his new bride and her two little boys.

That's the tale as I heard it. Tyler remembers a different story. Kelly and Cal's versions are different too, but everyone agrees that something happened at that old dark house. Something bad. They never found Halloway. Some say he drowned himself in the river after realizing what he had done. Others say he still wanders the woods near the house, the same blood stained axe in his hand, waiting for his wife to return – or others like her.

Suddenly the lane seemed even darker and the wind, whispering through the hedge, colder. We lowered our voices and edged closer together.

"I hope we find the river soon," whispered Kelly. It was what we were all thinking. I didn't think there was much chance of sailing any further now that cloud had blotted out most of the moonlight but it would have been nice to be in the boat again, under cover.

Suddenly Tyler stopped and raised his hand to silence us.

I thought he was listening for the river.

"I thought I heard something," he said.

"The river?"

"No."

"What?"

"Someone. Behind us, I think."

We all glanced round, but it was too dim to see anything but shadows.

"Pack it in, Grey," Kelly said sharply.

"I *heard* something."

"So who'd you think it is, Ty? You think it's old Bill Halloway, out for his evening stroll?" Cal joked.

Tyler shrugged.

Cal snorted and struck a match. The lane came alive with shadows – but only for a moment, then the darkness fell again as suddenly and surely as if someone had switched off a light bulb in a room without windows.

We started moving again. From somewhere behind us I thought I heard a branch break, then quickly told myself that it was probably some night creature, a badger or fox on its usual hunt for food. Yet in my mind I saw the tall, dark shape of a man with an axe, its blade glinting red in the moonlight.

More steps. More noises.

This is how it went: I heard a twig snap, looked around, saw nothing. The grass in the field behind the hedge crunched. When I stopped to listen I heard nothing more. This, for half a mile or so. Then the others, Tyler first, then Kelly, Ben and finally Cal began to notice things too.

A snap. A crunch. A slosh. A *murmur.*

We froze in our tracks.

"It's him!" one of us shouted. Tyler, I think, though I'm not sure. My heart was jumping in my ears.

Another murmur drifted out from the blackness. It was low and rumbling. Tyler took a step backwards and his heel cut into my shin.

"Maybe it's a dog or something," Ben whispered, but there was no conviction in his voice. Dogs sound like dogs. People sound like people. We all realized this. There was somebody else with us on that dark lane. Somebody big by the sound of the heavy footsteps. Bill Halloway was a big man; he'd grown himself big cutting trees, building walls, digging graves.

Then there was no sound, but I turned anyway and suddenly he was there. Tall, dark, shadowy. Moving slowly towards me like Frankenstein, like Dracula, like the worst thing you could possibly wish to meet on a dark, October night. That's as much as I saw. After that I fought the dizzying urge to faint and found myself running, following the others. Thorns tore at our arms and legs when sudden turns in the hedge surprised us. Potholes in the ground twisted our ankles and large stones barked our shins. But we kept on running, until finally, when our hearts were pounding fit to burst, we allowed ourselves a look behind and there was nothing but blackness.

"He's gone," gasped Kelly.

I noticed that the hedge, too, had gone, and the farm fields; they had petered into wasteland.

"We lost him." Ben giggled uneasily.

Tyler picked up a flat stone at his feet and launched it in the direction we had come from, shouting at the top of his voice, "Big fat ugly-looking murderer, you didn't scare me." And now that the heat was off we fell into fits of nervous laughter. I fell against Ben and shook so hard I could hardly breathe, especially when Cal began mimicking Tyler and his hysterical cries of: *It's him. It's him. It's old Bill Halloway.*

I suppose right then we were all too relieved to be cautious any more, and that's why we didn't notice *Him* return. At least not for a while. Not until he was almost upon us, towering like a huge dark monster from a late night horror show. I had sunk, laughing, to the ground, which now felt hard and stony, strewn with more of those flat pieces of rock Tyler had launched at the ghost. Cal had his back turned, helping to steady Kelly as she pulled a thorn from her ankle. It was Tyler who saw Him first. It was his scream that sobered us. But right then we were lost – miles from home ground, and all the rules of home ground combat. Like little kids, we all just froze.

Except for Tyler, who panicked and ran. And the man, ignoring us, called out and ran after him, muttering hoarsely.

I tried to stand but it was as if all the blood and strength had drained from my legs. They tingled but I couldn't move them. Kelly was pulling herself up on her knees, looking confused and frightened.

But there was no fear in Cal at that moment – at least not for himself. Almost as soon as the man charged past him, Cal had realized what was happening and he turned and ran too, scrambling and almost falling in his hurry to get to the man before the man got to Tyler.

I don't know how long it took, but I finally got to my feet – by which time Ben and Kelly had clicked into gear and were chasing after Tyler, too.

I cried out, but nobody heard. My voice had dried up. "Don't hurt him. Please don't hurt him." I felt useless. A sudden rush of tears made me almost blind.

"Save him," I cried and finally my voice came back. It tore through the night like the squeal of fingernails drawing down a black-board. And from the blackness a sound came back. A scream. A cry. A commotion. I heard the scramble of feet, the clapping sound of falling rocks and then, worst of all, silence.

As I stepped forward and the moon broke free of the clouds, shapes began to appear. Odd shapes. Wrong. Ben and Kelly were sitting on the ground, Ben's arm around Kelly's shoulder. She looked shocked and upset. A few paces ahead of them, Cal knelt in the dirt, gasping. And ahead of Cal, just ahead of him, I saw the man. The man had Tyler in his grasp. That's when I snapped. I leapt at the man, tugging, pulling, trying to free Tyler. I couldn't understand why the others weren't helping.

It took both Cal and Ben to pull me off. Cal was yelling, "Stop it, Jack. Stop!" But I continued thrashing, trying to break free. I was confused. Everything was wrong. Instead of helping me, Cal and Ben were pulling me away. And now Kelly was yelling too, "It's all right, Jack. He's OK."

It took a while for me to understand what had happened and it wasn't anything anyone said that explained the situation. It was when my vision finally cleared and I looked out over the edge of the deep dark ravine and saw how close Tyler was to the edge of it, that I realized.

The old man wasn't out to kill us. He was

coming to warn us. If Tyler had kept on running, if we had continued walking blindly along that lane, one of us, or two, or maybe all of us would have fallen to our deaths.

CHAPTER TWELVE

The old man was called Elzevir. He was a gipsy and had been heading back to his camp after a day touring the area looking for work and trying to sell his carvings, when he had heard us on the disused lane. Something in our voices, our careless tone, made him think we were strangers to the area. The locals show more respect to the region south of the river, with its deadly pits and potholes, and the man-made hole of the quarry. Few venture that way after dark without good cause. Elzevir was an exception. He was born in the area and knew the country and its short-cuts well. He told us that we couldn't have been further from the river than if we had plotted a route by the stars. We must have taken a wrong turn almost as soon as we set out from the town. If we hadn't been lucky enough to run into Elzevir when we did, and if Tyler hadn't done a nose-dive into the quarry, we'd probably have wandered right off the map.

Elzevir advised us not to carry on tonight. His camp was not far away and we could rest there.

"Rest," Kelly said, dreamily.

"Rest and eat and in the morning you will continue your journey refreshed."

The camp wasn't quite what I thought it would be. I guess I was expecting at least a horse and a caravan. Actually there was nothing but an old canvas tent and a couple of pots and pans next to which lay the powdery remains of a stick fire. But then nothing much these days seemed to be the way I expected it.

Elzevir pulled a plastic cigarette lighter from his pocket and a clutch of dry wood from beneath the groundsheet of the tent, and soon we were squatting on plastic bags around a crackling fire, watching a copper pot of what looked like brown volcanic lava come to the boil. The fire took the night chill away and made me feel warm and happy and one of the family. For a time I forgot the reason we were there. When I was younger my father press-ganged me into the same scout troop he had been in as a boy. During the six months I stuck it out we sometimes had camp-outs and bon-fires, and this was kind of similar, but with one important difference: this time, I was there because *I* wanted to be there. That's what makes nights like this special, and rare. You can't fake them.

While we were waiting for the lava to warm through, and Tyler began making thick doorstep sandwiches out of the bananas and peanut butter we had bought from the super-market, I apologized to Elzevir as best I could for what happened in the lane.

"... I don't normally do stuff like that," I added, because sorry didn't seem quite enough. "It's just that I ... well, you know, I thought you were somebody else."

Elzevir shrugged, then exchanged glances with Tyler and pinched his cheek the way everyone over a certain age seems to want to.

"Jack thought you were Old Man Hal-loway," Tyler laughed, handing Elzevir the first monster sandwich. He lost no time in making me look stupid. Unbelievable, I know: you risk your life for someone and...

"I thought you were very brave." Kelly smiled at me, the firelight making her eyes smile too.

Very brave!

"Late," nodded Cal. "But brave."

I had to apologize again a moment later, for swearing. I don't normally do that. Not in company anyway.

The lava was great – and not just because right then a dead horse on a stick would have been welcome. It really was good. Kind of thick and dark and salty, like the wholesome stews I remember my mum making for us a few years ago when Dad didn't work late so often and she wasn't so busy with her badminton and WI meetings; when we were a real family instead of one of those deep-frozen, fast food families you see in glossy magazine ads for microwaves and dishwashers.

The fire burned down quickly to a skeleton of glowing embers. Cal went to fetch more wood.

"Your friend," Elzevir poked at the dying fire with a stick and then threw it on to keep the ashes burning, "seems a little ... troubled."

"Cal? Is it that obvious?" I asked. "I thought it was only me. People say I worry too much about him."

"Eyes," Elzevir whispered. "They tell the tale. You can slap on a smile. You can shrug your shoulders and lie quite perfectly – but the eyes, they never lie."

I thought about Cal's eyes for a moment. They were deep, moody brown – almost black. Their dark brows were often pulled together and down into what could almost have been a frown, except I think there was actually more confusion there than anger.

"His brother died a year ago," Kelly told Elzevir. As always, something uncomfortable churned in my stomach. It would be wrong to say that I still couldn't believe it. I'd lived with the fact every day for over a year. But I still found it hard to accept that we were still here and he had gone, and that everything carried on the same. Just the way it would have done if it had been Cal or Kelly or Tyler or me.

"Cal built a motor bike and someone stole it," Tyler said. "We're going to get it back. It means a lot to Cal."

"Problems." Elzevir nodded as if he'd known all along.

"Maybe," Ben was staring at the old man's hands, "you could look at his palm. Tell his fortune."

Elzevir shook his head. "Don't need to. I've learned enough, just by looking, just by listening. You can learn so much about folks this way."

"Like what?" I shuffled closer to Elzevir and the warm glow of the dying fire. "What can you learn?"

"For instance?" Kelly pressed.

"For instance." The gipsy narrowed his eyes at Kelly and then dropped his gaze to the shapes she had, without knowing, scratched into the ground at her feet. Soft, flowery swirls and water wave patterns. "You, young lady, are going to be a fine artist some day. That is, if a handsome young prince, besotted with your beauty," he looked at me and tipped me a crafty wink, "doesn't steal you away before-hand."

Kelly looked at Elzevir as if he had just given her the answer to a question that had been troubling her all day.

"What about Cal?" I broke the silence that followed. "Can we help him?"

"Yes."

Silence again. Then I heard the wind gust beyond the dark line of trees.

"How?" I pressed the old man. I wanted an answer, some magical prescription that would put everything right again. For over a year I'd searched and failed to find one. "I need to know," I said, almost pleading. "All I can do at the moment is watch him and listen and steer him away from trouble until he finds the answer himself."

Elzevir nodded thoughtfully. A moment later Cal came back with his arms full. He threw a dozen sticks on the fire and handed the rest to Elzevir.

"Did I miss anything?" he asked, as the wood began to hiss and crackle in the flames.

"Kelly's going to be a great artist," I said.

"So what else is new?" Cal replied, then went on to tell Elzevir about the wonderful pictures Kelly had painted at school, some of which now hung in the Barn.

We had been talking quietly for about five minutes – Ben asking Elzevir if it really was possible to find your way across country with only the stars to guide you, because all his previous Scout masters had needed a pretty good compass and map – when Tyler got up and began mooching round the campsite, turning over stones and poking around with a piece of the firewood. For as long as I can remember Tyler has never been able to sit still for long, unless he's squatting in front of a TV screen watching Tom get another thrashing from the little mouse and the big dog next door.

Now Tyler pulled out of his pocket the Superball he'd traded Ricky Hawthorn two newts for, and began tossing and catching it. It suddenly struck me that I'd never seen him miss a catch. Never. No matter how high or wide he threw the ball. When the Superball lost its appeal Tyler popped it back into his pocket, and after a little shuffling and searching, pulled out his harmonica.

A moment later music began to drift through the clearing. "Piano Man", I think. An old Billy Joel song.

Campfires and music go hand in hand. Add to these, food and friends, the best of each, and you begin to realize that paradise doesn't have to be some sun-drenched tropical beach a million miles from home.

"You study music?" Elzevir was obviously impressed.

"Naw. I taught myself," replied Tyler, passing the harmonica to Elzevir.

The old gipsy blew into it once and the high screeching note that blared out reminded us just how good Tyler actually was.

"Can you teach me?" asked Elzevir. "It would be quite an achievement. My wife would be so surprised. She loved music. All kinds. 'Greensleeves' was her favourite." He hummed a little of the tune.

"You're married?" I asked, surprised.

Elzevir nodded.

I looked round the campsite but saw no sign of a woman's touch.

"Is your wife with you?" I asked.

"I like to think so."

"But –"

"Izabelle died thirteen years ago. Very quickly. Peaceful."

"But you just said she was…"

"With me? Yes. Oh, not all the time. Even when we were together we needed our space. That's why we travelled, see? But it's my guess she's keeping an eye on me. Making sure I'm not drinking too much. She didn't like that. Or smoking – but I can't seem to kick that habit." His gaze drifted into the fire and he smiled to himself. "Oh, she's going to give me such a hard time over it someday."

Elzevir stopped and looked up from the flames. I suppose it was our bewildered

146

expressions that encouraged him to continue.

"All that stuff about 'till death us do part' is wrong, you know. It goes way beyond that. Things move too fast these days. People only believe what they see. Do you understand?"

I was reminded of a book I'd once read about a man who'd been killed in a car crash and told his tale to his brother through a psychic medium.

"I think I understand," said Ben.

"I'm not sure," murmured Kelly.

Elzevir placed his forefinger on the ground and drew a line in the earth. "People," he said, "think everything is a straight line, with a beginning, a middle and an end. But those who have kept in touch with the earth, those who understand the old ways, know that there are no straight lines. Just circles. Wheels within wheels, constantly turning."

A moment later Elzevir showed us that the line we thought was straight had actually been curved as, with one easy movement, he continued with the line and turned it into an almost perfect circle.

I looked at Cal. He was gazing into the fire. Nobody spoke for a long time. Nobody needed to. The silence was broken by Tyler, who picked up the harmonica and began playing "Greensleeves", and although I'm sure he hadn't played the tune before, he played it perfectly. At the end of the tune Tyler handed the instrument to Elzevir, who attempted the tune himself.

"Oh, dear me," he shook his head apologetically.

"It'll take time," smiled Tyler. "You've just got to work at it. Pick it up as you go along."

"*Everything*," said Elzevir, looking at me, not Tyler, "*takes time*." Then he turned to Tyler, and as he held out the harmonica to him, said, "I suppose nothing great is easy. It is simply that great artists make it seem so."

Tyler did not reach for the harmonica. He stared at Elzevir for a moment, then said something that surprised us all: "You keep it."

I guess it was Tyler's way of saying thank you.

"I shall treasure it." Elzevir ran his long fingers over the shiny surface as if it were a precious stone. "And each time I look at it I will remember this night and you all here – *special*."

As the fire died down, our talking did too. By the time the last burning stick crumbled into ashes, Kelly, Ben and Tyler were asleep, protected only by their coats and the line of trees that kept us from the wind. I suppose after the day we'd had and all the walking we'd done, we could have slept just about anywhere. Cal and Elzevir were still talking quietly as I drifted off. The weather was kind to us. There was no rain or wind or thunder to break our rest – or if there was, we all slept through it.

I was the first to wake, at least the first of the Barnstormers. Sometime before I rose Elzevir had trampled the ashes down, gathered up his pots and pans, and packed away his tent and gone. At first, still sleepy and a little confused, I wondered if Elzevir had really existed, or whether last night had been a dream. But then, as the morning bleariness left, I noticed scratched into the flattened patch where the tent had been pitched, these words:

NEVER BE FOOLED BY WHAT YOU THINK –
IT'S WHAT YOU *FEEL* THAT COUNTS.
GOOD LUCK
E.

The sun was high and the wind, for the moment at least, had taken itself and most of the grey clouds of yesterday someplace else. Back up river maybe. Over our town. Probably over Hadrian's Academy and the Barnstormer's new school. The week before I was set to go to Hadrian's for the first time, my brother was confined to bed recovering from chickenpox and I was worried about having to go there alone. I asked Cal where it was and how I could find it. He said, "Just look for the black cloud, Jacko. If there's a

149

school anywhere around, it will be directly beneath it."

He was right too. It rained that day. I remember it clearly. I suppose everybody remembers their first day at any school. It thundered and rained and I was among a hundred people and yet completely alone. My brother was at home and my friends were a million miles away, in some big modern comprehensive school. I was sure I'd lose them there; they'd be swept in through its big entrance doors with a thousand other kids, and they'd meet and mingle and I'd never see them again. Up until the accident, that night before my first day at Hadrian's was the worst of my life.

CHAPTER THIRTEEN

The fox was standing on the prow when we finally made it back to the boat, but it leapt inside for cover as Tyler hopped aboard with the ease of an old sea-salt and called, "Splice-the-mainbrace and shiver-me-timbers," in the best pirate voice he could muster.

"Half a day on the water," moaned Cal jokingly, as he climbed carefully aboard, "and he's Long John Silver."

Long John Silver replied that Cal was nothing but a scurvy-riddled sea-dog.

The scurvy-riddled sea-dog thumped him.

Mutiny is an ugly thing to witness. Cal whipped his leg around the back of Tyler's leg and Tyler literally hit the deck.

"Fight!" Kelly shrieked.

"Fight!" Ben and I repeated, wasting no time in diving aboard. And suddenly it was a just-like-the-old-days, every-man-for-himself

151

scrap. I can't really say much else about it because I didn't have a very good view of the situation. All I know is that almost immediately I dived aboard I was pinned to the deck; someone had my arm twisted up my back high enough to worry me. I had hold of somebody's leg and there was a thumb in my ear and it was neither of mine. Eventually I managed to twist around so that my arm wasn't hurting so much, and somehow this one mass of arms and legs broke into two. Cal was still latched on to me like a terrier with a rat. Kelly and Ben had shuffled away and were gaining the upper hand of Tyler. There was a small home-made life ring hooked to the side of the boat and I tried to get to it. I wasn't sure what I was going to do with it – it just seemed like a good idea at the time to grab it. But it was no use. I just couldn't reach it. Even though I'd twisted round I still wasn't able to break free. Every time I moved, Cal moved too and countered it perfectly. The boat had been rocking wildly during the fight and I began to feel queasy. In the end, worried that there might be a reappearance of the broth I'd shared with Elzevir the night before, I gave up the fair fight, twisted enough so that Cal would counter, and when he did so and leaned his weight on me again, I fell back and screamed like my arm had just been fractured in several places.

Everybody froze, everybody except me. I

took the opportunity to grab Cal by his shirt, pull him off balance and use the gathering momentum to hook my knee into this chest and roll him over the side and into the river.

Five minutes after splashdown, we were cruising again.

Kelly took the tiller. Cal, still shivering slightly from his mishap, rowed. By rights I suppose I should have felt a little guilty. The river this late in the year is cold enough to take your breath away. But I didn't feel guilty. I didn't feel bad at all. Even with half his clothes draped over the side of the boat and the other half still damp and sticking to him, Cal looked comfortable here. Happy even. I suddenly realized I hadn't seen him smoking, a habit he'd picked up half a year ago, since before we ran into Elzevir. I felt happy too. My grandfather, when he visited us on holidays, used to spoil me rotten. Mum always frowned at this, but Grandad would toss her a long-toothed grin and ruffle my hair and declare, "What can I say? When *he's* happy, *I'm* happy."

I never really understood what that meant until then.

It was Tuesday. We should have been back by now. Back in school.

But it wasn't just Tuesday. It was Tuesday the thirty-first.

Hallowe'en.

None of us had really thought about it until Tyler, scratching our names and the day, month and year into the deck of the boat with the blade of his rusty penknife, reminded us. It's odd that we'd forgotten. Other times it would have been important. Normally, we'd have spent the day plotting some evil trick to spring on the junior school crowd during their usual after-school party; one good fright for Hallowe'en.

Later that day we were passed by a smart little cruiser, headed up river towards our town. We were all above board, including the fox which, as I was taking my turn with the "oar", was nuzzling into one of Tyler's enormous sandwiches. Cal had to jerk the tiller to pull us out of the cruiser's path. Its name, painted on the hull in fine red letters, was *Utopia* and the guy at the wheel looked like an older, fatter Charlie Brown wearing a captain's cap.

"Ahoy, there!" he bellowed as if we were at either ends of the Suez canal. He jabbed a stumpy finger behind him. "There's a fine nor'-easter coming over. I'd batten down the hatches if I were you."

As the boat swept past us, I called, "We're fresh out of battens."

"What are battens anyway?" asked Tyler.

"Something to do with relay running," grinned Ben.

154

"Bet he's a teacher," mumbled Cal, as the boat moved on. Cal reached into the bag, pulled out another sandwich and then looked at it with disgust. He, like the rest of us, had overdosed on them and Elzevir's lava the night before. Like a fisherman with a catch not worth the effort, he threw it back into the bag.

"No," I said, watching the boat get smaller as it moved up river. "A carpet salesman."

This was a game we sometimes played.

"Librarian," Ben suggested.

"Clerk," said Kelly.

"Bank manager," added Tyler.

As we all gazed back at the cabin cruiser and the boring little teacher-salesman-clerk who'd become too small to see clearly, Cal whispered, "God, I hope none of us end up like that."

The replies were loud and clear.

"Not me."

"No way."

"You must be joking."

"I'd rather die."

"What the hell is a fine nor'-easter anyway?"

"Good question."

"Who cares?"

It was sunny and the wind was warm. One of those strange October days that remind you that although winter is driving towards you in the fast lane, summer is only a moment behind. That fine nor'-easter was hours away and the warning signs, if there were any, would go unnoticed right up until the fast-gathering clouds turned black.

We spent the next hour on deck, playing cards as the boat continued its lazy drifting, helped by one of us taking a turn with the piece of wood Cal had brought along as an oar. Tyler had brought the cards. There was a character in a comic I used to get called Pete and the comic-strip was called "Pete's Pockets". Pete had these bottomless pockets and whenever he got into trouble, whatever he needed would be in his pockets. You name it. A mousetrap. A hammer. A Sherman Tank. If Pete delved deep enough into his pockets, he'd find it. Tyler was like Pete. I think he carried everything he owned, or at least everything he cared about, around with him. One day, when we were in the same registration class at junior school, our teacher's fountain-pen went missing and we all had to turn out the contents of our pockets on the desks. Tyler ended up with a pile of junk that looked like a sculpture of Mount Everest. From his trousers he pulled a penknife, a compass and magnet, a rubber band catapult and five ring-pulls from the special free-gift cans of Coke. From his jacket he brought out his Superball, three chewed Biros, a theatre playbill, a collection of football card swaps (he didn't collect them but they came in handy if some kid who did had something Tyler wanted) a water pistol, some change and the mouth organ he later gave to Elzevir. But no fountain-pen. It was eventually found, two days later, under the radiator behind the teacher's chair!

We played poker mostly. If we'd been staking money on the game I think Cal would be a pretty rich kid by now. He's so good at it because you can never really tell what he's thinking or whether he's bluffing. Me, if I get more than a pair of sixes I begin to beam like it's the first day of summer, and everyone folds. But the game was fun. There was no hassle. It was good just to sit there losing a fortune in unreal money as the sun warmed our backs and the fox, as the water sloshed the sides of the boat, climbed over us trying to find a comfortable position. All thoughts of home and school and Corman had left us way down river. Only occasionally did the wind gust cold and remind us of the Halloway House and the real reason we were doing this.

At around tea-time, when the final preparations for the Hallowe'en bash back home would have been well under way, as the sky began to darken, we reached the landmark that told us the Halloway House was no longer a dream: it was the old Bellman pottery, which on our map had been shown as a row of three one-shaped towers on the south bank of the river. Two of these towers still stood intact; the crumbling third, furthest downstream, looked like the ruins of some besieged castle from one of the glossy history books they have in the Hadrian library. If the scale of our map was right, the old Morton Cut – the lane which would lead us from the river through the forestry land to the old house – was only a few miles more. The Halloway House was now close enough to wake the moths in our stomach and start them fluttering again.

I looked at my friends, but nobody said anything. Nobody had to. The silence said enough. No jokes now, not even from Tyler. This was for real. We were miles from home, it was Hallowe'en and we were closer to the house of our nightmares than we had ever been in our lives. I glanced up from the boat and noticed for the first time that things had changed. Sometime, while we had been on deck talking and playing cards, the loose patches of cloud had darkened and crept over the sky like a grey patchwork quilt, and that "fine nor'-easter" the guy in the motorboat had warned us about was beginning to whip through the riverside trees. Beside me, Tyler reached into his back pocket for the harmonica (playing it was something he did in times of stress) but of course it wasn't there. Instead, he leaned into the carrier bag and took a bite of another sandwich. Only a small bite. Not one of Greg Tyler's best efforts. There was no enthusiasm in it.

"When we get back," he said with a curled lip, staring at the piece of bread queasily, "I'm never going to look at another peanut butter sandwich as long as I live."

I think it was the only time ever that we all agreed with what Tyler said.

The old Morton Cut was like a ghost; like something you think you catch out of the corner of your eye, and then find you are wrong. Now that we were close, we saw it everywhere, then as we drew nearer to the suspected area we realized that it was just a trampled patch in the riverside weeds, or some other abandoned footpath. Not our cut. The path we were looking for was sign-posted Morton Forest, from a time when the river was still used as a means of transport and the path ran through the woods to the village of Castleton, a further eight miles inland.

"It's getting dark," murmured Ben, looking up at the thickening clouds. The sun was quite low now and the clear patch of sky to the left of the river was striped with orange and red. In an hour or so, clouds or not, it would be black as pitch.

I was watching Kelly sketch the fox on a weather-worn part of the deck, when suddenly the boat began to rock, sending the fox scrambling to Cal for cover and causing Kelly to lose control of the pencil she'd been using. Instead of having a neat foxy mouth, the portrait wore a broad Cheshire-cat grin. It was Tyler who'd caused the upset. "Stop the ship!" He leapt up, almost screaming. "There it is! There it is!" He was jabbing his finger at another bare patch in the bank about a hundred metres ahead of us. Ben climbed to his feet, causing the boat to sway again, and looked to where Tyler was pointing.

"What is it?"

"It's the cut. Put the brakes on."

"I don't think so," whispered Kelly, sliding the pencil back into her pencil case and pushing it into her pocket.

I was thinking of backing Kelly up, but as I've said, Tyler did have the knack of proving people wrong about these things. Ben, who wasn't yet familiar with this fact, said, "I don't see any signpost."

"Yeah," I agreed. Suddenly the odds seemed better. "No signpost." I looked at Kelly and tipped her a wink.

"So what do you call that, Romeo?" cried Tyler. I strained to see where Tyler was pointing, but all I saw was a fallen branch or pole or –

"A signpost," Cal said coolly. And as the boat drifted nearer, I stared at the leaning, mossed-over sign with just one thing on my mind: what did Tyler mean, "Romeo"?

Had I been staring at Kelly? I didn't know. I wasn't sure. There seemed to be so much I wasn't sure of lately. I wasn't sure about home or school. I wasn't sure if I could talk to Cal any more. And I wasn't sure if Kelly had always been beautiful, or if she had suddenly changed, duckling to swan, overnight.

"I can't see," I heard Ben say. "*Is* it a signpost?"

"No!" cried Tyler. "Not *a* signpost. *The* signpost."

And he was right.

Morton Forest it read, although if we hadn't known the name it might have been difficult to make out. The post had given in to the weather long ago, allowing years of hot summers, damp, misty autumns and frosty winters to crack the paint and eat into the wood beneath. I suppose if the cut had still been in use, the sign would have been replaced with a weather-proofed iron one like some of the others we passed, but the old Morton Cut, like the signpost that marked it, was something from another age; a relic forgotten by everyone but the school kids who still talk about Old Man Halloway and what he is supposed to have done.

This time we didn't bother to camouflage the boat after dragging it up on to the reed bank. No one, we decided, would come this

far downstream who wasn't a serious boat-
man and therefore somebody who would find
our shabby little boat something best to be
avoided. Looking back at it from the start of
the Morton Cut I wondered how it had managed to get us this far without sinking. It was
good, I thought as we began walking, to be on
solid ground again.

The first spatters of rain came as we were
about fifteen minutes into the cut. We heard it
before we felt it, splashing on the falling leaves
of the wild-growing bushes that were beginning to take over the lane. At certain places,
branches either side of the lane clawed at you,
so that my trousers were no longer simply
dirty. Now they were thorn-cut and snagged
too. I knew this for certain, although I could
barely see them. Night had fallen fast. Even
with the moon peering out of the broken
clouds, without the street lamps we were all
accustomed to, it still seemed very dark. What
light there was appeared to make the shadows
blacker than black. The wind had become
colder too. A strong, whistling night wind that
would have been comfortable if heard from
the safety and warmth of a bedroom window.
The fox, walking alongside Cal, like a dog
walking to heel, stopped a moment to shake
water from its coat. Flicking the collar of her
school coat up, Kelly looked up at the sky and
said, "I wonder if it's raining back home."

"Doesn't it always," replied Cal. It was a statement, not a question. But Tyler answered it anyway.

"It never used to."

"You never remember the times it rains," I put in, just to keep things balanced. "You forget."

"Rain or not, I don't think I'll ever forget tonight," murmured Ben.

I didn't think I would either.

As we moved further into the lane, I began to think again of the Halloway House and what we could expect to find. I thought about ghosts and evil and all the tales we had heard over the years, but on a more down-to-earth note, I wondered if we really would find Lightning there. The idea that we'd been set up crossed my mind. Maybe that new kid had planted that note in my pocket to win a place in Corman's gang. I was finding it hard right then to believe that anyone did anything simply because they thought it was the right thing to do. Of course, by now the house might be just a pile of rubble. In a way, I hoped it would be. It had been an old house even when Halloway went ape with the chopping axe. Maybe it had been pulled down. On the other hand some rich couple from the city might have bought it and turned it into a weekend place. That's been happening a lot lately. Some of the locals have been getting angry.

"Maybe it's gone." Tyler put words to my thought. He and Ben were walking ahead of us now. I noticed hope in his voice as he said it, the way hope would creep into his words when he would say, before a history test, "Maybe Mr Sumner's ill. Maybe they'll cancel it."

I felt Cal shrug beside me. "Nothing lasts," he said quietly.

Kelly, who had been keeping step with Cal and me suddenly quickened her pace until she reached Tyler and Ben, who were now so far ahead as to be just dark outlines in the distance.

"Was it something I said?" Cal looked at me with a half-serious frown.

"Listen, Cal," I began, looking down at the fox, wondering what had happened in its life for it to be alone. Cal stared at me with the same puzzled expression he'd been wearing lately and listened, but all he heard was the steady patter of rain on the leaves. Sometimes, when you're thrown a simple question quite suddenly, your mind fills up with so much junk you're left confused and speechless. That's how I felt right then. I didn't know how to continue. Looking at Cal in the moonlight, with his hair no longer slicked back but tousled and wet, I thought he looked younger than he had in years. In fact he looked like Toby. I remembered something then, that came as a shock: Andrew Calahan was actually three months younger than me.

Cal tilted his head sideways. "Listen to what? I don't hear anything."

"No." I shrugged. "I don't either."

I looked down at my muddy, scuffed school shoes, thinking hard as we continued along that dark lane in silence but for the wind and rain. Then an idea came to me. A good idea. A solution. I grabbed Cal's arm and pulled him to a stop and he looked at me, startled. I was gripping his arm so tightly it must have hurt. "Listen, Cal," I began, but what I saw behind my friend wiped clear from my mind whatever words had been on my tongue. The house, standing there surrounded by a tangle of sick-looking trees, made me think of a big black spider in the centre of a giant web. It seemed to be waiting for us. Waiting and watching. I'd forgotten the reason we were there. I couldn't imagine any reason important enough to enter this building. It looked like the dark old mansion on the cover of a paperback horror story; tall and twisted with a garden of dead weeds and shattered windows that frowned down on you like the dark eyes of an ancient scowling face.

I heard Tyler swear under his breath. He, Kelly and Ben had frozen in their tracks as soon as the house had come into view. Cal and I almost ran into them.

"It looks..." Ben searched for a word

worthy enough for such a building, but gave up.

"Haunted," whispered Kelly.

"If this were a movie, there'd be a flash of lightning now," Ben breathed with awe. "There'd be thunder and lightning."

If this were a movie, I thought to myself, *I'd hand back my popcorn and walk out of the dark theatre into the sunlight.*

CHAPTER FOURTEEN

Slowly, we moved into the house's shadow and found ourselves at the foot of the garden. The house had once been surrounded by a neat picket fence, but most of this had fallen. The pieces that were left leant one way or another, making the few pieces of wood that remained perfectly upright look wrong. A leaning "For Sale" sign stood among the weeds like a mouldering hangman's gallows, while at the house ahead of it, tatters of curtain flapped out of the jagged holes where the windows had been.

"You know, if we turn back now maybe we'll get home for breakfast," Tyler said. He said this lightly, but I think deep down he was hoping that one of us would agree with him. He looked at Ben, probably because Ben had been the least keen of us to see the Halloway House. With Ben there had been no real curiosity about the legend we had all grown up with – no history. It was clear that Tyler's suggestion appealed to him. But then Ben glanced at Cal and this seemed to sway his decision. Maybe deep down he really wanted to see what was behind that rotting door. Or maybe he was thinking of a way to show Cal that he wanted to be more than an outsider with a temporary pass into our group. "No," he said crisply. "I think we should go in."

And so, cautiously, nervously, reluctantly, we did.

As we started along that overgrown path, something darted at us from the dark eves of the house. "Bats!" Kelly shrieked, jabbing a finger above us while shooting to her knees a split second before the rest of us. She was partly right. A bat. Just one, that's all. But by the time we had all straightened up and caught our breath, we found to our surprise that we had reached the house.

I wasn't sure what the chances were of finding Lightning in there. I wasn't sure if it really mattered any more. The thought that we had been set up crossed my mind again, but I didn't really care. I just wanted to get in there and out and back home as soon as possible.

The door was open a crack. Just enough to allow someone, I thought, to peer out at us. Without a word Cal spread a hand on the peeling wood, looked at us and then pushed on the door. It swung halfway open with a low cree-

creee-eeeek that made me feel sick. I think it was more than just being scared. Something about finally being at the Halloway House, the place we'd so often, as little kids, talked about going to when we were older, made me feel both sad and frightened at the same time. Time had moved on. We were older. Things had changed. Only once before in my life can I remember wanting to be someplace else more that I did now. That was on the lakeside just after Toby's accident. Except then I didn't just want to be someplace else. I wanted to die.

"Tell me again," I said half joking – half serious, "whose idea was it to come here?" Right then, Lightning or no Lightning, it seemed the craziest thing we'd ever done. It was so shadowy in there, so weird, that even Cal hesitated before entering. From his pocket he pulled out one of the half melted candles we keep in the Barn and lit it with the third damp match he tried.

Out on the path, the flame spat and flickered wildly, but once in the passage of the house it settled a little and grew taller. With my heart beating double time I followed Cal into the narrow, musty hallway and felt the others shuffle in close behind. The horrible festering smell inside made me wish I was standing next to Kelly and her sweet perfume. There was someone close behind me and I knew it was Tyler. I could feel his hand gripping my

169

shoulder – something I would normally shrug off, telling him to act his age. But this time I didn't. Truth is, I was glad to feel it there. It made the sickness in my stomach subside.

The hallway we had entered was long and narrow, strewn with broken glass and mouldering leaves. I picked up the fox so that it wouldn't cut its paws on the litter. On the right were the stairs leading up to the next level, while to the left, at opposite ends of a damp-stained wall with peeling paper of a big, flowery, old-fashioned pattern, were two doors. The door our end of the corridor, two rectangular panels top and bottom, was closed. The farther door was the same except that it was open a crack; like the front door, as if someone was in the room, spying on us. I had heard of people saying they *felt* as though they were being watched. That's exactly how I felt.

For a moment it was as if we had all become showroom dummies. Only our eyes moved over the dark cobwebby walls. I thought the door along the hall creaked, but then I realized the sound had come from the stairs. Kelly was standing on the first bare step of the rotten stairway, looking up to the dark landing. Tyler was staring at her, his eyes big, wide and worried. "Kelly," he whispered. "Don't!" His grip on my shoulder became painful. "That's where they say it happened."

"This place is a wreck." Kelly nodded up to

170

a gaping hole in the ceiling at the top of the landing, where rain was dripping in.

"Come on, Cal," Tyler said. "We've done what we said we'd do. Lightning isn't here."

"Just a quick look around," Cal said evenly.

The open door at the end of the hall led into what had been the kitchen. An old-fashioned, cottagey sort of place. Big enamel sink under greasy window, a couple of painted wall cupboards, an ancient-looking cooker and a table covered in dust and cobwebs that looked like the table Toby, Cal and I had dragged out of Oakley Beck years ago. There was just one picture on the wall: a print of a boat on a lake beside a thatched cottage. When I got closer I saw that it was a calendar. The year was nineteen sixty-three. More than a lifetime ago.

Finding nothing monstrous in the kitchen eased all our minds and made pushing open the closed door along the corridor easier, but the thing that leapt out at Cal as soon as he did so reminded us just where we were and got our hearts beating at a respectful pace again. Tyler began to giggle nervously. He jabbed a pudgy finger at me as if I'd done something incredible. "It's only a rat, Jack-o. No need to jump like that."

"I didn't jump," I said shortly.

"You kinda did," said Cal.

I looked at Ben.

Ben glanced at Tyler and Cal, and nodded.

171

"You nearly hit the roof," he said, smiling and following Cal into the room.

It was a dull room. No motor bike. No ghost. Just a bloated leather sofa and two similar chairs. Smashed window. Tattered curtains. Broken TV. Upturned coffee table. Leaves. Cobwebs. Mould. Dust. And a terrible animal smell that made me want to spit.

Tyler spun round suddenly. "What was that?"

"What was what?"

"I thought I heard something."

This sounded familiar.

"Where?" asked Kelly as if she hadn't believed him.

"Upstairs."

"Stop fooling."

"I'm not fooling. I heard something."

"I didn't," murmured Cal.

"Me neither," added Ben.

I hadn't heard anything myself, but I felt the fox in my arms twitch just before or just after Tyler spoke. I wasn't sure which.

"Stop it, Greg, you're scaring the fox," I said sharply.

"I'm scaring *you*, you mean."

"I'm not scared."

"Then go upstairs. Where it happened."

I must have paused.

"Chicken."

"Shut up!" I shouted, then tried to get a grip

because any minute now I'd get the chicken impressions and I didn't want to blow my cool.

"Let's go," Ben said uneasily.

"Baaawk ... baaawk..." began Tyler.

Now Cal and Kelly were not just sniggering, but laughing. I saw Kelly grab hold of Cal to steady herself, and I spun round to face Tyler and opened my mouth before I knew it.

"Oh, go and drop dead, you fat little bastard."

The silence that followed was painful.

There are lines that are drawn as you get to know people, different lines for different people – friends, family, neighbours, teachers. Saying those words right then, the first five, not the last four, something that before the accident wouldn't have mattered, I knew I'd overstepped it.

I pushed the fox on to Ben, snatched the candle from Cal, spilling hot wax on to my hand, and started up the stairs. If a tour of the entire house was what was needed to get us home quickly, I decided to get it over with. To hell with Corman and Lightning, to hell with Halloway and his bloody axe. I just stormed up the stairs. At the top, a choice of direction made me stop. There were four doors, all covered in moss and mould. All slightly ajar. There was no broken glass here, and yet something glinted on the floor. For a moment I thought it was water, then realized that it was thicker and darker. It hung on the carpet rather than sank into it.

"Blood," whispered Kelly, who, followed by the others, had crept up behind me. Cal brushed past and squatted before the pool. He touched the liquid, rubbed it through his fingers and smelt it.

"Is it?" I heard Ben behind me say, and over this I thought I heard something else: a soft shuffling sound from one of the rooms. I couldn't tell which. Rats, I supposed. More rats. Terrific!

"Oil," answered Cal with a frown that deepened as he noticed something in the doorway of the furthest room. He signalled me to bring the candle closer. In the dimness the thing in the doorway looked like the winding skeleton of a snake, but as we got closer and Cal eased open the door I saw that it was a thick chain, another little pool of oil spilling from it like blood. Just ahead of it was a foot pedal and next to that, I could just make out the shape of a headlamp. It was Lightning! The bike *was* here, but in a hundred or more pieces, spread around the shadowy dark room like an exploded diagram from a workshop manual.

"It's true," murmured Kelly. "Corman really was here. That new kid was telling the truth."

I'm not sure if Cal heard. His eyes were

sweeping over the room, counting the pieces, taking stock, rebuilding the bike in his head.

"This is nuts." I shook my head. "If Corman wanted the bike so much, why'd he go and do this to it?"

"Because he's crazy," replied Tyler.

Cal stepped carefully over several smaller pieces of Lightning towards the darkest corner where what looked like the main frame of the bike was resting against the wall.

"I'd like to get my hands on him," spat Tyler, "for what he did to our caretaker. He's a nice bloke. He gave me some records once and now Dave Milligan says that since getting caught in the fire Corman started at school he's been in a coma."

I was about to point out that Dave Milligan was so full of it that the sewers were jealous, but something happened that made me freeze. The motor bike frame fell to the floor with a clatter that sent all the other pieces of the puzzle rattling like peas on a drum pad, and Cal was staggering backwards, trying to keep from falling. There was somebody else in the room! He'd been there, crouched in the corner, maybe watching, maybe sleeping. It might have been talk of the burned caretaker that startled him, or just Cal reaching for the bike frame behind which he hid. I don't know for sure. I really didn't know what was going on until I saw the two of them fighting. It was so fast and wild and unexpected that nobody moved until they had pushed their way across the room and out on to the landing. It was too dark to see anything clearly. But one thing caught the candlelight. Something bright. Something silvery like the blade of old man Halloway's axe. Tyler saw it in the same moment as I did. He screamed and without thinking ran out on to the landing, crying, "Stop it! Leave him! Stop it! Stop it!" They moved, the three of them, like a single shadowy mass and it all happened so fast. There was a sound of a punch retching the wind from someone, bone hitting brick, the clatter of metal on wood and then, worst of all, terrible, the earthquake rumbling sound of someone falling heavily down the stairs.

Then there was silence.

Like someone in a dream, I carried the candle on to the landing. Cal was leaning against the wall shaking his head dizzily, breathing as if he had just sprinted half a mile. The other boy was gasping too, hunched over on his knees, supporting himself with his hands. He looked up, blood trickling from his lip, his eyes wet with tears. He looked so small and young that for a moment I didn't even recognize Corman.

Kelly and Ben scrambled past me and down the stairs to where Tyler had fallen. Corman groped for the piece of metal that had been knocked from his hand. It was Lightning's handlebar, which he offered to Cal like a spoilt child giving up a toy he'd screamed for and now felt too guilty to keep.

"I don't want the bike," he said in a soft, strange voice.

Cal left him holding the handlebar, and as I scrambled down the stairs after him the day on the lake came back to me all too clearly. The scene at the bottom of the stairs was almost identical, except that it was Tyler's still body lying there, not Toby's. His face was white and his eyes were closed and blood was running in three thin streams from a cut on his forehead, just above his right eye.

"Not again!" My mind screamed so loudly I almost fainted.

Not again. Not again. *Not again!*

I looked around, my eyes hazy with tears. Ben had lost the colour from his face and sank, still holding the fox, to his knees. Beside me, Kelly steadied herself by slipping an arm around my waist and rested her head on my shoulder. I pulled her close, found her hand and squeezed it, all without thinking. Right then I couldn't think of much, except how strange it was that Cal, who back home had been spinning out of control, was the only one who remained calm and composed. Among the broken glass and leaves he squatted beside Tyler, lowering his head close, his ear to

Tyler's mouth, listening. It was something an adult had done to Toby that day at the lake.

"Is he ... is he all right?" I heard a voice say, a strange voice; not mine, not Ben's or Kelly's: Corman's. "I didn't mean to hurt him. I didn't mean to hurt anyone. He shouldn't have been there, that caretaker. Until Richy said what had happened, I didn't know he was there. I swear..."

"The caretaker's going to be OK." I said the words my mum had said to me after she had spoken to the school secretary on the telephone, just to shut him up, then looked down on Tyler again. "Cal, how is he?"

Cal pulled back a moment and slipped off his coat. "Breathing," he rasped as he rolled his coat into a pillow and gently slipped it under Tyler's head. "He needs a doctor. We'll have to find the boat again. Drift it down river to the next town."

"That's Harlow," cried Kelly. "Further than we've come already – and it's miles in from the river. Don't you remember the book? The map?"

"Overland then," said Ben. "There might be a farm."

"I'll go." Cal was already heading for the door when the strange unfamiliar voice came again. This time it was stronger and closer. Corman had climbed to his feet, crept downstairs and, still holding the metal bar, was looming over us, when he said forcefully, "No!"

Because all our maps showing the Halloway House were from Kelly's gran's books, all of which were almost as ancient as the old girl herself, we hadn't known what Corman was about to tell us: *that there was a road* – a good road cutting through the woodland about a mile from the house. It had been built around the time our Barn was abandoned, to traffic goods from the potteries and mills that had become factories and electronics firms as time went by and the river ceased to be a viable transport route. There were always trucks passing – even at night, said Corman.

Kelly and Ben stayed with Tyler, and although I wanted to be with him too, I tagged along with Corman and Cal just to make sure they made it to the road without ripping each other apart. It was hard going because most of the fields had been ploughed, and the wet clay stuck to our shoes in great clumps, making them feel like heavy working boots. Several times I lost a shoe to the mud until I fastened the laces so tightly, they hurt.

Just when I was beginning to think that things couldn't get worse, it began to rain. Not drizzle. Not spit. I mean heavy, pelting rain; rain with a capital everything. I peeled off my school blazer when it began to feel as cold and

179

heavy as armour-plate, and left it dripping on a hedge that marked the start of a sloping field of knee-high grass. The grass was soaking. Crossing that field was like wading through water – but none of us complained. In fact nobody said a word. Cal and Corman were too absorbed in their work (and ploughing through that mud and grass was *hard work*) to say anything. Both of them had tramped on ahead of me and I had to throw in all my effort just to keep them from getting away from me completely. In the darkness I couldn't tell who was Corman and who was Cal. They looked the same. I prayed they wouldn't start fighting again.

At the end of the field was a soaken hedge, broken just enough in places to allow you to squeeze through and get only minor cuts and scratches. Beyond that hedge was another field of long grass. This one so vast that you couldn't see the end of it. The ground here was even harder to walk on because the earth was looser and more uneven. But each time I felt my foot slip and twist into a chilly pool, I thought of Tyler lying at the foot of the stairs of the Halloway House, blood streaming down his face, and I surged on.

It was the feel of it under my foot that told us we had finally found the road, because in the darkness it was invisible. After the dips of the fields, and the grass and the mud, it seemed unreal – no not unreal; temporary. As if the road were a scratch in the land that would eventually heal and fade away. I don't know how long we waited there, standing in silence as the rain continued to pour, before the truck came rumbling like some mythical beast that belonged more to that dark landscape than we did. It rolled up behind us, spraying rain and belching smoke, moving fast. It roared past, so close it clipped my outstretched hand. The wind from it took my breath away. I leapt back, swearing at the two red lights that became one and then none before the burning in my fingers eased.

A long time later, hours it seemed, with no let up in the rain, another truck rolled up, drew level with us, then thundered past.

Without a word, we began to walk.

"Next truck," said Cal sometime later, "is going to stop."

The trucks, I think, were on a schedule, because it was the same long wait before the next one came along. The rain had thankfully eased to a thin drizzle by then, but it still blurred the truck's headlights and made its speed difficult to judge. It appeared to be shooting along the road like a bullet.

"It's not going to stop!" I yelled.

"It'll stop." I felt Cal nod certainly in the blackness.

"It can't even see us." My voice was small

181

next to the roar of the engine. The noise told me that the truck was close now. I could hear water spraying out from the tyres like sizzling fat, and faintly over it I heard someone cry, "It *has* to stop."

Within seconds the truck was close enough for me to see that it was different from the other trucks that had passed. It was newer and bigger. For a moment I thought I glimpsed a ghostly white face high up in the cabin, but then it was gone and out of my mind because something happened, something that, like the day at the lake, will stay in my mind, and every time I hear the screech of brakes it will come back to haunt me.

Suddenly, there was movement beside me. Cal, I thought, because Cal did crazy things, leapt into the road, directly into the path of the truck, madly waving and shouting for it to stop. But it wasn't Cal. It was Corman. I realized this when Cal himself dived into the road a split second after Corman, a split second before the truck driver hit the brakes.

It's hard to say what happened next. My memory of it is hazy; blurred by rain and dazzled by headlights and masked by the blare of a horn and the scream of brakes. And of course, my pounding heart. I thought it was going to burst.

The truck squealed to a halt in front of me. There was big lettering on its side, but most of

182

this was hidden by dirt sprayed up from other passing vehicles. I could only make out the last three letters – AXE.

Things began to haze. I remember the truck, like the biggest thing I'd ever seen, blotting out the entire world. I remember trying to move my feet and finding that fear had rooted them to the spot, knowing that Cal and Corman were dead because there had been no time for them to get out of the way; and it had been an age since the truck had screamed to a stop and nothing had happened. And I remember the sickening wave of dizziness that came as I thought of how Mrs Calahan would react when she was told her other son was dead too. After that there was nothing but blackness.

Then the blackness went.

I was in a room, small and white. There was a brilliant light, and a man was leaning over me. He had clear blue eyes and a beard that made him look like Jesus. *I was dead too,* I thought. *The truck must have skidded out of control and rolled off the road.*

Then I had the strange feeling that the room was moving, floating, like the boat. The man moved, and I saw that he was leaning over somebody lying opposite me, shining the same bright light into his eyes, and slowly everything came to me.

I was in an ambulance. It was Cal lying opposite. His right arm was in a kind of inflatable plastic tube. The left side of his face was scraped and bloody. I tried to say, "Are you all right?" But it came out "arrooo-orrrighh" and my head began to swim.

Cal nodded carefully, then shut his eyes in pain. Sitting next to him, near the door, I noticed Corman, his wet hair matted to his forehead, a bloody cotton pad held to his nose. He looked different. Changed. I wanted to ask more. I wanted to know about Tyler, but each time I opened my mouth my vision clouded and pain cut through my head like a million volts. I fell back and let the ambulance take me someplace else. They told me later what had happened: that I had fainted and clunked my head hard on the roadside. Neither Cal nor Corman had been hit by the truck as I'd thought – although if Cal had been a second or so slower chances are neither of them would have lived to fight again. Except they didn't fight any more.

Corman received nothing more than a few scratches and a bloody nose. Cal landed more awkwardly and broke his arm. I didn't know it at the time, but Tyler was in another ambulance about fifteen minutes ahead of us. He had a fractured skull. He hadn't regained consciousness by the time we reached Hartford General Hospital. There was talk of coma and brain damage but, even before our fraught parents showed up, he'd startled the intensive care unit by fluttering his eyelids and drunkenly murmuring, "It's a fine, fine, life…" which he later told us was a line from the musical *Oliver*. A local theatre group was planning the show as their New Year production and Tyler had been thinking of trying for a part.

Slowly, things drifted back to normal. Tyler got a month off school, which was twice as long as Cal. I managed to fake blinding headaches for a week and then was sussed when Mum came home early one day and caught me playing an old Ramones album loud enough to shake the plaster off the walls.

Of course we all got roasted by our parents, who took every opportunity they could to remind us how badly we screwed up and that we really weren't as grown up as we obviously thought we were. They couldn't believe we had drifted a dangerous, museum-piece of a wreck all the way down river when there was a perfectly good road we could have cycled down in half a day.

OK. Next time, we said, we would cycle. But we never did.

None of us returned to the Halloway House. As far as I know, Lightning is still there, still in pieces.

Mr Dobson, the school caretaker, got better quickly. Luckily for Corman, local gossip is bigger on sensation value than it is on fact, and in reality he suffered not much more than blisters and smoke inhalation. He returned to school the same day Cal did.

It was nearly six months later that Corman set foot in the place again. He got twenty-four weeks in the new juvenile detention centre out on Oakley Moor, about fifteen miles from the Halloway House. This sentence was shorter than it could have been because Corman owned up without anyone pointing the finger. And he needn't have done. Only we knew the truth and I don't think any of us would have spilled it. Not even Cal.

It would be wrong to say that after what happened Cal and Corman became friends. But at least when Corman returned from Oakley there was no more fighting. Both Cal and Corman trod the streets of town more quietly after that night at the Halloway House. Maybe they had learnt something. Maybe we all had. Or maybe it was just that things were changing.

I'm sure that Ben feels more like an insider now. Last week he and Cal enrolled for karate lessons run at the community centre by a couple of the cops Cal had earlier stretched to the limits of their patience.

Kelly has grown her hair longer and is prettier than ever. The fox still visits us and we always keep some food in the Barn just in case. But lately its visits have been less frequent. I have a feeling he's found a friend of his own.

Tyler got a part in the New Year show. The Artful Dodger. He was brilliant. We all went to see him on opening night, then Kelly and I returned together two days later. Our first real date.

It's strange, but not so long ago I was worried that things were coming to an end.

Now I feel as if they're only beginning.